The Called

Rahman Reuben

PRESS

This novel
is dedicated to
Jah-el,
the God of Abraham,
Isaac,
and Jacob.

Book 1

The Called

TABLE OF CONTENTS

PROLOGUE

Greetings, dear reader!

It's no accident that this book is in your hands. God's calling you!

To all who are already members of "The Called" (*Christians*) you already know there's no coincidence in Christ. That said may your reading make your spiritual ears even more acutely aware of His continual knocking at the door of your heart, to a re-calling of your first love passion toward Him and His will (Rev. 2:4–5; Rev. 3:19–20). That of loving Him with *all* of your *all* and of loving your fellow-man as yourself, most particularly in individually proclaiming His saving gospel of grace to this lost and dying world (Matt. 28:19; Luke 10:17; Luke 14:23). We already know hell is real and that grace has a grace period, and it's our commission to make that plain to the unsuspecting!

If you're a non-Christian and are about to take this literary journey I can tell you that He's calling you to earnest repentance of your sins, by acceptance of His Son the Lord Jesus Christ as your only means to personal salvation (John

3:16–18; Acts 2:21; Rom. 10:9–10). I pray your eyes will be opened by God the Holy Spirit to the love, kindness, and mercy of God the Father, and that you'll answer His call to you via this publication. A short prayer as to how is provided in the Epilogue; but do feel free to answer Him at any time in your reading!

An important part of my *calling* is to help you see God, to facilitate you to better understand the mysteries of the Bible, to equip you to better traverse the correlation between the Old Testament, the Gospels, and the New Testament (including the Revelation), in this enlightening, entertaining, and exciting new way. And lastly, to enable you to better comprehend the reasons behind the supernatural war raging ever more intensely today between the invisible forces of good and evil. May your imaginations be empowered by God the Holy Spirit to see the story/plan of the Father, by the Son, even more vividly via this publication.

Thirty percent of all royalties to this author from this book are cheerfully and obediently relinquished, to the Raymond R. Rochester Foundation for Christian Philanthropy as a first fruits offering to God. This Fund is a "Joseph Generation", wise stewardship, start-up ministry dedicated to the diligent pursuance of God's Kingdom and His righteousness on Earth, by increasing the Master's talents and giving as Holy Spirit directs to the funding of the three C's; Christ's Church, Commission, and Charity to the poor (Pss.37: 25; Prov. 3: 9,10; Prov. 19: 17; Matt.6: 19-21; Matt. 6: 33; Matt.25: 20,21; Matt. 28:19; Luke 6: 38; Luke 12: 33,34; Acts 20: 35; 1 Cor. 4: 2; 2 Cor. 9: 6-15; Phil.4: 19).

Jesus is due to return, and I believe it much sooner than most think! I also believe with all my heart that this book will be instrumental in the final calling of His souls to harvest! This is my step of faith, and I pray it will be instrumental in igniting yours (Heb. 11:1).

You that hath an ear may you hear what the Spirit is saying—Amen.

FOREWORD

I am Enoch.

I am the teller of this story,
the history of man.

I saw the vision of the Holy One in Heaven
which the angels showed me,
and from them I understood and I saw,
but not for my generation,
but for a remote one far to come.

Your generation.

CHAPTER 1

BEFORE THE BEGINNING

He that is eternal is eternity. He that is infinite is infinity and is Alpha and Omega , the beginning and the end. It was in this infinity before time as we know it, that there was the Godhead—the Trinity—three parts equaling completion and completion equaling three parts. Omnipotent, omnipresent, and omniscient They are He, and He is They, an eternal mystery escaping the narrow intellectual boundaries of those who cannot hear His call, the ever-present source of all that He caused to be—the Father of the called. He who was, is, and always will be, the almighty and eternal Spirit.

He who upon the advent of time by the fall of man into the corruption of sin would become known as the Lord of spirits, the Head of days, the Ancient of Days, Jah-el, the I AM that I AM, Adonai, Elohim, Yahweh, and finally Jehovah, the Father.

He who upon the advent of time by the fall of man into the corruption of sin would so love His crowning creation (man) that He in His omnipotence would humble His all-powerful person to the point of revealing Himself intimately. By trividing Himself would He also become known as the Word, and Wonderful, Counselor, the Mighty God, the everlasting Father, the Prince of Peace, the Lamb, Immanuel, Yeshua, and finally Jesus Christ, the Son of man, the Messiah.

He who upon the advent of time by the fall of man into the corruption of sin would also become known as the active force, the Comforter, the Holy Spirit, the dove, and the cloven flame of fire who leads the called from the birth of time to its death. At the finish of His plan will time return from whence it came, back to the dust of eternity. He was alone, and in His infinite wisdom He decided that this would be no longer.

There was nothing. There was *no* thing. Nothing spirit but God Himself. Nothing corporeal, for its existence was in the purpose of God for a future time. This would not be the state of affairs for much longer. The plan of God was formulated; He had decided, and so would His will be done. Even though God the Father knew aforetime that there would be one of His spirit creations who would cause chaos in all His creation, He would create anyway. For the entities that He would create, both spirit and corporeal, would have the right of exercising freedom of choice. There was one to arise out of His spirit creation that would exercise this freedom in error. One who would cause a crack in infinity, the birth of time, and the corruption of His soon-to-be crowning creation—man. Thereby did the Lord God, prior to His creation of anything heavenly or earthly, solve this future diabolical dilemma by reaching within Himself. God the Father said unto God the Son,

"Prepare thy Self, for I have in mind to create that we shall no longer be alone. But alas, there shall arise one from amongst our heavenly creatures who will mislead them who will be of corporeal creation, man, whom We shall create in Our own image. For there shall be enmity between Us and this spirit that is soon to be. You will know him by his exceeding pride, and it shall prove to be his downfall. Therefore, let Us prepare Ourselves for a future time when We shall have to suffer separation. For in all eternity We have been One together. But for Our crowning creation, for Our image, must it become necessary to reveal the mystery of Us. For out of this chaos shall conclude a battle between the sons of light and the sons of darkness. Many shall be called of Our crowning creation to hearken unto Our voice, but few shall heed. It is for those who answer that We will be separated and revealed. At My appointed time must You become My chosen, My Lamb slain before the setting of the foundation of the world."

God the Son, knowing full well that God the Father is all-knowing and all-powerful, questioned not, but accepted His will.

The Lord God said, "Let Us create for Ourselves a dwelling place!" And whatever was the decree of God the Father, He spoke to God the Son all that was to be of Their heavenly dwelling place. In turn, God the Son spoke the will of God the Father unto God the Holy Spirit, and whatever God spoke into being was brought into existence. The Lord God created for Himself structure beyond the length, breadth, and depth of human imagination. He created a structure beyond immensity, to serve as the vestibule before the main entrance of His house. This vestibule is built like unto crystal, and the walls of it like crystals hung as tassels. The walls shimmer with the radiant white cool light of a crystal exposed to light, and also with rainbow-colored spectrum brilliance. The floor of the vestibule is like unto sheet crystal, and the marriage of floor and walls in the presence of the Most High dance with every color of the spectrum in dazzling mixture. This vestibule is electrified, pulsating, and luminescent; its many entrances aglow with luminosity, for it is the entrance to the house of the Lord of light. In its ceiling, the height of which cannot be described, is the activity of what appears like shooting stars in spectacular abundance, in the midst of lightnings of every color imaginable and unimaginable. The entire vestibule is an activity that reflects the holiness of the Ancient of Days, upon His entering and exiting. God gazed upon His handiwork, and smiled upon its perfection.

The Lord now turned His attention to His main structure, which He spoke into being as His primary abode. Inside this house is such vastness that its apartments are as mansions without number to accommodate His spirit creatures, and those corporeal who would heed His future call. The incalculable number of grid-like boulevards between these complexes appear as though paved with pure gold. All, from each direction, converge into a main central court of praise. Within this court the Head of days placed His throne, for it pleased Him that He should now be revered, worshipped, and adored. The area of the great court surrounding His throne, in the midst of this house, is so vast that in future times, by His prophets, it would become known as the sea of glass. This is the palatial structure of the King of kings, and the Lord of lords. This house far exceeds the magnitude of the vestibule that houses the gigantic main entrance through to the broadest boulevard that empties into the court of praise. This house is indescribable in splendor, extent, and magnificence. Its floor is like unto clear glass, and its ceiling like unto the ceiling of the vestibule, but in far more exceeding excellence. Such is the heavenly inanimate will of God. His dwelling place is holy, perfect, and without blemish, and would remain so throughout all eternity. Now had arrived the time for God to speak into existence His throne of power. Here He would take His seat, and speak into existence further things seen and unseen.

The Lord stood upon the sea of glass, in the immensity of what was about to become His throne room and spoke, "Here is My throne!" And in an instant, out of nothing, it appeared before His presence. The throne was lofty in appearance, and it sat upon an expanse of enormous space, and was supported by four wheels within wheels. These wheels pulse the colors of citron green, turquoise, yellow, pastel pinks, and the pure cool white of crystals shining with brilliance. These wheels are of such great height that they are dreadful in appearance, and each wheel is full of eyes round about. Above these wheels hovered the enormous crystal expanse which supports the throne of God. From below the wheels issue their pulsating hues of greens, turquoise, yellows, pinks, and pure white light in startling crispness and clarity as the reflections of diamonds, sapphires, emeralds, and beryls in pure white light. Above the wheels, on the surface of the expanse on which the throne of God sits, these same colors emanate, but are slightly muted by the suspension distance between the throne expanse and the wheels. The throne itself has the appearance of a shimmering sapphire, radiating the color of a deep and royal rich blue. The Lord God thundered, "I am upon my throne!" and immediately He was there. He sat upon His seat of authority, fixed upon the crystal firmament that hovers over the four wheels within wheels. He peered out over the sea of glass below. He took in the sights of His pulsating and glittering structure, His heavenly city. He lifted His almighty head to the expanse of the ceiling of His house and perused all activity within. The entire house gave honor, praise, and glory to the Alpha and Omega, for this structure reflected His perfect light wherever He went.

God sat upon His throne and spoke into being a high wall of crystal, pulsating and flickering in brilliance and luminosity, as the appearance of flaming fire. This wall completely surrounded the perfect heavenly habitat of the Godhead. With the kingdom of heaven completed, the Lord God prepared Himself to speak into being its inhabitants and subjects. God the Father then said unto God the Son, "Say this unto God the Holy Spirit. Create the heavenly beings as spirit, as We are. They shall be Our servants, and the servants of those soon to be created in the corporeal, Our image. They shall glorify and magnify Our name forever in Our presence. Before this throne, they shall be called angels."

God the Father, God the Son, and God the Holy Spirit, He who is the will, He who speaks the will and He who creates the will. The source, the course, and the force is God, the three divine and eternal luminaries who are complete only in three, and are therefore one in the light.

God the Holy Spirit set into motion with ease the will of God the Father. He created angelic forces in number like the sands of the seas. He created them cherubim, seraphim and ophanim. Of the cherubim He created two kinds, those with sixteen wings, and those with twenty-four. The cherubim with twenty-four wings are those angelic creatures who are closest before the presence of God. The function of their wings is that with the uppermost eight they must hide their four faces; with the intermediate eight they must fly to and from the presence of God, and with the remaining eight the tips must tuck under the soles of their feet. They cannot look upon the face of God because of its exceeding brilliance. They cannot stand upon the crystal expanse on which His throne sits, for it is most holy. They are God's guardians of His holiness, and therefore equipped to move in His presence. God also created the six-winged seraphim for the same purpose, although they are single-sided with faces like unto eagles. These are the cleansing agents of God. The Lord would use them far into the future in bringing death upon Egypt and Assyria, and to remove any whom He chooses to cut off.

The cherubim with sixteen wings are of a lesser rank than those with twenty-four. They stand on the sea of glass below the throne platform, or fly in the great hall singing and shouting praises to the Most High God. From these the Lord God chose four to place amongst the four wheels on which His throne is supported. These cherubim are called forth whenever He would depart the kingdom of heaven. The throne platform God created is mobile. The cherubim with the sixteen wings can hide their faces before God. They can fly before His presence to receive short-term instruction, but they cannot stand in His presence on the expanse surrounding His throne. Whenever the Lord God wishes to pilot His throne chariot, He summons the four cherubim of the wheels.

The cherubim are four-sided creatures. All have a body like unto a man on all four sides, and all have four faces. Their feet are straight feet as unto hooves, and the soles of their feet are like the soles of a calf's foot, and their feet sparkle like polished brass. Their wings are six to a side, and are joined at the top of their shoulders at all four sides, but in layers of three, and fold over one another when at rest. Underneath their wings, on all four of their sides, they have the arms and hands of a man. When they move they dart in straight lines up, and down, north, south, east, and west. If looked upon from all four sides, on one side is a face like unto a man, on the other a face like unto an ox, on another a face like unto a lion, and on the final side a face like unto an eagle. Their appearance is like burning coals in a fire, and like the appearance of lamps, and their bodies crackle with the appearance of perpetual lightning.

God had now become the Creator and He had created ten thousand times ten thousand, and thousands of thousands of angelic creatures. He set them in rank, and file, and order. The ophanim are the more numerous of His heavenly hosts. Over the ophanim He appointed the sixteen-winged cherubim. Over the sixteen-winged cherubim He appointed the seraphim. Over the seraphim He appointed the twenty-four winged cherubim. Amongst these latter He created the archangels Michael, Gabriel, Raphael, Uriel, Raguel, Saraqael, and Remiel. These are they who would soon come to be counted amongst the good angels, and leaders of the sons of light. He also created Semjazael, Arikabael, Rameel, Kokabiel, Tamiel, Ramiel, Danel, Ezeqeel, Baraqijael, Azazel, Armorosel, Batarel, Ananel, Zaqiel, Samsapeel, Satarel, Turel, Jomjael, and Sariel. These are they who would soon become counted amongst the sons of darkness, those that would soon fall from grace, into corruption and darkness, by following mutinous Lucifer.

The Lord God had completed His creation of His inanimate heavenly kingdom, and was soon to be finished with the animate spirit creatures, His angels. He created them in three classes as He saw fit. He had created Michael, Raphael, Gabriel and Uriel. In the far distant future these four would become known as the four beasts who stand before the throne of His presence. He had created all that He had intended in His heavenly kingdom, with the exception of one. God at this point was about to create His crowning angelic being. This one was to be in appearance more spectacular than any of the other angels. It would be this angel's special assignment to be chief guardian to the throne of holiness of God. It would be he that would lead all the other angelic beings in the praise and worship of the Ancient of Days. It would be he that would be closest to the Most High.

The Lord God spoke into existence a cherub like no other. Only that of the Creator Himself surpassed his stature and presence in excellence. This cherub was exquisite in beauty. His appearance was like an intense pure white light shining through a tasseled robe made of every precious stone. He sparkled and glimmered the fiery crystal hue of the sardius stone. He shimmered in the hues of the beryl and topaz, yellows, greens, turquoise, and pinks. He shone forth in the crystal blackish green of the jasper stone, and the deep rich royal blue of the sapphire, his body a slow ever-changing mixture of patterns and colors. His hoofed feet and wings glistened with the burnished ocher of pure gold. The Lord God gazed upon His finished creation and said, "Thy name shall be called Lucifer, the son of the morning, the bright morning star. It is your station to guard My holiness, and to lead your brethren in the worship of Me, for I am the Most High God. I am the Ancient of Days, the Lord of spirits, the King of kings, and Lord of lords. I am Jah-el!"

Lucifer bowed low before Jah-el. He and all the other angelic beings had prostrated themselves upon the sea of glass. The Lord Jah-el spoke with His voice of thunder saying, "Lucifer, son of the morning! Michael! Gabriel! Raphael and Uriel! Rise up from your places, and come hither before the throne of Jah-el!" Lucifer stood first and said to Michael, Gabriel, Raphael and Uriel his brethren,

"The Lord God Creator summons us. Let us spread these mighty wings that He has seen fit to give us, and go hear His commands!" Each cherub's three layers of wings opened in unison to full extension parallel to the floor, making them appear as but eight, revealing their blinding bodies. At first the five angels flexed their wings in slow, tentative up and down movements. Then, as if by instinct, they increased them to a pace of beating that made them blur to the appearance of only four, and then so rapidly that they seemed to disappear.

As they rose into the expanse of the great praise hall it appeared as if they were floating. The remaining angels lifted their heads toward the great ceiling of the main hall. They watched as Lucifer and the four covering cherubim flew upwards toward the great distance that separated the sea of glass from the vast expanse on which sat Jah-el on His throne. As Lucifer and the four covering cherubim ascended past the indescribable proportions of the wheels of Jah-el's throne chariot, they heard the rumblings of His almighty voice anew. Jah-el decreed unto His angelic subjects, "You are My handiwork. It is by Me that you have come to be. I am God, and your Creator. Because of Me you have been brought into existence. I am your life. From this moment forward, and throughout all eternity to come, you shall be called the stars of Jah-el!" God the Father, God the Son, and God the Holy Spirit, together they are complete, and came to be known to their angelic creations by one name—Jah-el.

Lucifer was the first to reach the platform on which sat the throne of God; the remaining four cherubim following close behind this obvious leader. They streaked across the great expanse of the pulsating crystal firmament, towards the blinding presence that sat upon the royal blue throne. Instinctively their shorter, first layer shield wings separated them selves and encased their faces. Then their longer foot wings dropped into place, encasing their entire bodies as a shroud and wrapping the tips beneath the soles of their feet. Though completely covered, Lucifer and the four could still feel the penetrating bombardment of Jah-el's emanating deity and holiness. Jah-el, the greatest of light, the Father of light, for He is light, sat peering out at His approaching workmanship. Five powerful angelic spirit creatures were now standing before Him. They were beautiful indeed, especially the one called Lucifer.

Jah-el spoke to Lucifer and said, "Lucifer come hither." Lucifer lifted himself slightly aloft with his mighty golden wings and touched himself down before the very presence of God. Jah-el spoke endearingly to Lucifer, "Oh Lucifer, thy bright and morning star. I have created you for My pleasure and special purpose. You shall guard my holiness closely. You shall lead all your brethren in unceasing praise before Me. You are the chief covering cherub, and at your command I place a third of the stars of heaven your brethren. Be not wise in your own wisdom O Lucifer, and be not taken with thine excellent beauty, for you are My creation to do My bidding. Come and take your position on the left hand side of My seat of power." Little did Lucifer, nor any of the other angels, realize that Jah-el, who spoke to them as one, was in actuality three.

Jah-el commissioned Lucifer His chief of praise, but Michael He appointed His chief of might. Jah-el summoned Michael and said, "Michael you shall be known as the merciful, and as the archangel. Your name means *he who is like God*. To you I give charge over all the remainder of the stars of heaven, your brethren. Go now and station yourself on the outermost right front corner of my throne platform, station Gabriel on the far left front corner, station Raphael on the far right rear corner, and Uriel on the far left rear corner. You Michael are my military might. Go and do as I have commanded!" They lifted themselves aloft and touched themselves down, each to his assigned position. Lucifer felt a slight but fleeting pang of jealousy towards Michael's more encompassing leadership role, but he soon put it to rest in comparison to his own unique beauty and the special position he held in the presence of God. After all he stood at the left hand of Jah-el, while Michael was far removed to the chariot's corner.

Each of the five covering cherubim were now stationed in their place. These cherubim with their four sides and four faces were equipped and ready to do the bidding of Jah- el. They would go forth in future with their face like unto a man and attest to the mercies of God. They would go forth with their face like unto an eagle and attest to the swift wrath of God. They would go forth with their face like unto an ox and attest to the strength of God. And they would go forth with their face like unto a lion and attest to the royalty of God. The covering cherubim were complete. The seraphim and the ophanim were complete. The kingdom of Jah-el in the heaven of His dominion was complete. Jah-el would soon create dimension, matter, space, length, breadth, depth, height, and volume, dimensions necessary to support the corporeal, His crowning creation—Man.

Jah-el spoke to Lucifer by command and instructed, "Lucifer, son of the morning, lift up thy voice and call unto all your brethren who are bowed below on the sea of glass. Tell them it is nigh time that they should praise, worship, honor, and adore Me for their existence. For I am God!"

Lucifer lifted his voice aloud, and spoke as the blast of a trumpet all that Jah-el had commanded. The ceiling of the main hall became a spectacle of lightning movements before the throne of Jah-el. Ophanim filled the highest levels farthermost away from God's presence, and worshiped Him from a distance. For they too are one-sided creatures, having a face like unto a man, but have neither shield nor foot wings, but only wings of flight. Michael, Gabriel, Raphael, and Uriel were summoned from their extreme posts to just adjacent the throne. This to allow the twenty-four winged cherubim, and six-winged seraphim to stand upon the platform expanse, that they might worship Him as befitting of their winged privilege. For if Michael, Gabriel, Raphael, and Uriel are not drawn nigh to the throne of God, away from their sentry post, no angel in heaven is able to stand before the throne, for there is no admittance to audience before Him unless He calls unto Himself the four sentinel corner cherubim.

Lucifer enthusiastically led the praising of Jah-el. The outermost ophanim praised His holy name in one magnificent choral accord of angelic voices. The twenty-four-winged cherubim and the six-winged seraphim stood upon the platform expanse around His throne harmonizing, "Holy! Holy! Holy! Blessed be God the Almighty!" And the sixteen-winged cherubim flew around the throne, between the ophanim and the angels on the platform, extolling, "Blessed is the Lord God Jah-el, the Ancient of Days, and Lord of creation. For He alone is worthy of all praise, worship, and honor. For He is the life giver and Father of all existence." From that time before time the praising of the Most High began in the heaven of His dominion, and so it would be forevermore.

The Lord God Jah-el was well pleased with His creation thus far. He sat upon His throne relishing the adoration, as His heavenly hosts ministered unto Him. But still He was not satisfied. He had in mind to create a being that would be like nothing He had created thus far. His intention was to create a spirit being, encased in a corporeal shell. He had created all that was His intention in His heavenly dominion, and without any consultation with His angelic creatures, Jah-el spoke within Himself. He spoke to God the Son saying, "I have in mind to create a crowning creation, one that will be corporeal. We must prepare for him space and matter, a home, and a seat of his own authority. We will make him a little lower than the angels, but he will be made in Our image, a tangible tripartite reflection of Us. He shall be comprised of spirit, soul, and flesh. His race shall be called man, and he will become the father of all mankind. We shall call his name Adam. I will tell you all that I have in mind to do, and it shall come to pass by the Holy Spirit. I have designated our dominion the third heaven, the first dimension. And man's shall become known as the first heaven, the third dimension. Ours is the spirit realm, and theirs shall be the corporeal. Our heaven shall become known as the doorway, for it is the division between spirit and corporeal, between Our dominion and their dominion." The Lord God Jah-el was approaching the time of His creating a small blue and green sphere, in a galaxy amongst billions of galaxies. He was about to create additional heavens and earth, and all therein, and His jewel of creation—Man.

In the midst of all the angelic praise and adoration of the Most High, Jah-el commanded Lucifer to silence. Then there was silence in heaven. The Ancient of Days decreed to Michael the archangel, "Command the stars of heaven your brethren to lift themselves from before My face. Tell them to position themselves below me on the sea of glass, and I will show them marvels—and the marvel of marvels which I am about to create. When you have done My command then return you, Gabriel, Raphael and Uriel back to your post, for I am not to be disturbed." Michael did as Jah-el commanded.

When all of the heavenly host were in position Jah-el

proclaimed, "Stars of the most high, gaze toward the ceiling of this great hall and behold the magnificence of your Lord Creator Spirit." Jah-el then gave further private instruction to Lucifer to shield all but his face that is like unto a man, and cautioned him to not look upon Him. Lucifer followed explicitly all that Jah-el decreed. He recognized instinctively even without warning to not peer directly into the Shekinah of the Most High at such close proximity. And so with his face like unto a man he stared upward in curious anticipation. The ceiling had ceased its dazzling activity and was clear.

The angels at a distance could see that the perpetual blinding aura that Jah-el usually emitted had now become what seemed like a softened, dense, gaseous cloud. It was to the angels of heaven as if Jah-el had retracted deep within Himself, leaving Lucifer with the sense that the Lord of glory was no longer present on the throne platform. Without warning Jah-el's light, already the most intense that any angel had witnessed, resurged with unprecedented, spectacular brilliance. His throne room was aglow as never before. His presence was overpowering, overflowing, and all encompassing. The walls, and the floor like unto a sea of glass, were awash in all the colors of the rainbow, opals, and mother of pearl. The colors raced back and forth, to and fro, sweeping in waves over His entire house. The view from the outside made the city of God appear as one gigantic super nova emitting great long shafts of light from a core of pure cool white and ice blue. The shafts of light were pastel tones, intermingled with deep emerald, sapphire and amber—breathtaking colors without name.

Michael, Gabriel, Raphael, and Uriel stood firm at their assigned posts, with their shield wings clenched tightly over three of their faces. But with their face like unto the face of a man, they stared upward and away from whence came the glory of God. Jah-el was about to create as He had not created before. Lucifer, being the closest to God, heard things that could not be understood even by his own supernatural intellect. He heard thunders of three different pitches and tones. "No it cannot be. It must be due to the great surge of His power," Lucifer pondered. "Who can understand the mystery and might of the Most High Jah-el?" he questioned intimately. Indeed Jah-el had taught Lucifer and His myriads of the spirit realm many mysteries but not all, especially the mystery of the Godhead. But soon, even that mystery would have to be revealed.

Suddenly a great wide shaft of pure white light, originating from the sapphire blue throne, shot straight up through the immense expanse between the throne platform and ceiling. As it did, wide pulsating rings of pure white energy rippled from the central source of that power. The angels of heaven stood aghast, transfixed in their places like statues. Little could any of them realize that Jah-el was in actuality—three. Lucifer had not even the slightest inkling that the three pitches of thunder were in actuality the conversation between God the Father, Son, and the acknowledging Holy Spirit. Neither could he perceive that the super awesome force rumbling forth from Jah-el was in fact the Lord Creator Spirit, the active-force, and power of the Godhead.

Jah-el was creating. He had spoken within Himself. The angels watched in amazement as the pure white light of Jah-el punched through the ceiling expanse and began creating a massive portal in the first dimension through which would come the birth of the corporeal. In the third heaven the Holy Spirit created the alpha portal. This is the doorway between the spirit realm and the corporeal. At this point is the inner dominion of Jah-el's kingdom. Jah-el gave the command within Himself, and the Holy Spirit burst through the portal fixed by Himself in the third heaven. He rushed through the portal in an ever-widening arc, radiating in every direction from the mouth of the alpha portal. As He did He spewed forth all that the Father had commanded, through the Son. He spewed forth space and filled it with galaxies of pre-stars, solar systems, and planets. Amongst these was a small molten mass of matter that would soon become known as Earth, the third planet from the sun.

The Holy Spirit continued His push forth in His ever-increasing and widening arc. In a circle He perfectly turned back upon Himself, and fixed the omega portal in the third heaven on His returning side. The Holy Spirit, by the Father's command, made the kingdom of heaven the beginning and ending place of the finite world.

By radiating Himself outward, and circularly in all directions at once through the alpha portal, and returning to Himself through the omega portal, God the Holy Spirit created space. Jah-el had projected, and returned to Himself, to create the continuum of space. To retract the finite world all Jah-el would have to do is command the Holy Spirit to release Himself from the omega portal, and redraw into Himself through the alpha portal all that occupies His created space. At this point where the beginning and end, the alpha and omega merge, is the inner dominion of Jah-el's kingdom. The procession through the alpha and omega portals of the third heaven will bring anyone entering to the beginning and ending consecutively. The beginning of all things is Jah-el. The finality of all things is Jah-el. The third heaven is the inner sanctum, the point where all things end and begin.

Up to this point there was no need for space as we know it. Jah-el and the spirit realm do not exist in the third dimension of space, but in the first dimension of spirit. Jah-el is infinity. There was nothing in comparison to something, as we humans would come to define something.

In this new creation of space Jah-el continued. He created the divisions of the heavens. He created in the finite world the division between the third and the second heaven. In the beginning God created the heavens. Now had arrived the appointed time of Jah-el to create the earth and all therein. Jah-el had fixed the boundary of the finite world from the portals of the third heaven to the end of the second. This is the second division.

The planetary and galactic bodies of the second division of heaven were fixed and would not alter their stations. Jah-el is perfect order, and across the billions of light years of this division of finite heaven, there was no chaos amongst these heavenly bodies. Within the outermost rim of the finite second division, Jah-el caused a great and massive galaxy to appear, a galaxy that far into the future would become known as the Milky Way. It is in the very center of this outermost rim of the finite second heaven that He caused the Milky Way to be. In this galaxy amongst all others was a small and seemingly insignificant solar system made up of nine planets rotating around a dark pre-star. This was the solar system amongst all others that contained the planet that would become home to the marvel of marvels.

This outermost rim of the finite second division was thousands upon thousands of light years in breadth, and housed innumerable galaxies. Proceeding outward beyond this outermost rim was nothing but the blackness of lightless infinity. There are no galaxies, no planets, no stars, just the vacuum and continuum of zero space. Jah-el gave this space of the second heaven no boundary, but from its creation it has continued outward, and is still continuing. Jah-el fixed in this infinite second division of heaven all of the galaxies of stars, planets, and wonders which define finite space.

In the middle of the outermost rim of the finite second heaven, a rim that is in breadth one seven-thousandth of the entire depth of the finite second division, is the galaxy of the Milky Way. In a nine-planet solar system, on a seemingly insignificant orb of molten matter soon to be called Earth, Jah-el would shortly create the creature that would be made in His image. In view of all that Jah-el had caused to be since it had pleased Him to begin creation, it seemed an irony that a corporeal being, in a tangible setting, would become classified as His most miraculous creation. It was as Lucifer had wondered within himself previously, "Who can understand the mysteries of Jah-el?"

The ultra-spectacular display of God ceased and He returned to the brightness of light that His angelic hosts had grown accustomed. Jah-el reposed upon His throne whilst His heavenly hosts marveled at what was now before them. There was now an outside world. The angels, overwhelmed with awe, great joy, and admiration, began proclaiming in ecstasy, "Blessed is the great God and Creator Jah-el. There is none like Him. For He is the origin of all creation great and small!" The angelic servants of God were unrestrained in their worship of Him. Then the voice of Jah-el pealed once more from His great seat of authority saying, "Contain thy praises and adorations O servants of the Most High, for these are but the beginning of marvels. Now shall I make ready to reveal unto you the marvel of all marvels."

Heaven became silent once more. The angels gazed intently at the work of His hands. They trembled at the awesomeness of His almighty power. Heaven was silent in anticipation of this coming marvel of marvels.

CHAPTER 2

THE BEGINNING

The Lord God Jah-el turned His attention to the third planet of the nine-planet solar system in the galaxy of the Milky Way. This planet was at first a molten mass but the Lord God created upon its surface, water to cool its intense heat; the entire globe was entombed in water.

The earth was without form, and void; and darkness was upon the face of the deep, and the Spirit of God moved upon the surface of the waters. And God said, "Let there be light." And there was light. All of the galaxies of pre-stars became stars in their full sense. The entire universe of the division of finite second heaven lit up in its brilliance. Jah-el had spoken His light into the murky expanse of second heaven. All of the luminaries were aglow with His light, save that one which would soon become known as the sun. Its special light was to be spoken into existence shortly.

God saw the light that it was good, and God separated the light from the darkness, distinguishing light and darkness. And the beginning and the ending completed His first day of creation on the earth. God said, "Let there be a division in the midst of the waters, and let there be a division between the waters and the waters." Then God made the expanse, a division between the waters that were to remain on the earth's surface and the waters that were to be stored above the earth; and it came to be so. God called the expanse between the division of the waters heaven. In the midst of the second heaven around this planet Earth, God caused the first heaven to appear. This heaven was unique in that it was an atmosphere capable of sustaining corporeal life, and the marvel of marvels that was soon to be created. In the third heaven existed the spiritual realm. In the second heaven existed the finite world, and the vacuum of endless space. In the first heaven, housed in the second, would come to exist the realm of the corporeal. There came to be beginning and completion, and the second thousand-year *creative* day of Jah-el's work on Earth came to its close.

Jah-el had taken the water that He had separated from the surface of the globe and completely wrapped it around high above the earth. When He would come to create the vegetation of the earth, and give His light to the sun, this encasement of water would cause a greenhouse effect. The earth would be warm and tropical from pole to pole. There would be no snow or harsh winds. It would be a paradise throughout.

And God said, "Let the waters of the earth be gathered together to one place, and let the dry land appear." And it was so. And God called the dry land earth; and the gathering together of the waters He called seas, and God saw that it was good. Then God said, "Let the earth bring forth grass, vegetation full of seed, fruit trees giving fruit according to their kinds." And it came to be so.

The earth brought forth grass, and vegetation bearing its seed, and fruit trees bearing forth fruit according to its kind.

God saw that this was good, and there came to be beginning and completion of the third thousand-year-day of Jah-el's creation upon the earth. Michael, Gabriel, Raphael, and Uriel, along with their heavenly brethren sang songs of joy and praises to the Most High God. He was causing a new thing to come into existence, something wondrous and completely different.

Lucifer stood in the presence of the Most High, just a small distance from the source of all life. With his head erect, his eyes were fixed trancelike on what was occurring before him. Instead of being lost in the ecstatic praising of Jah-el wholeheartedly, as were his brethren, Lucifer's mind was accelerating with question upon question concerning the mystery and power of Jah-el. Lucifer was standing there, and before realizing it had formulated a vision of himself sitting upon the throne of Jah-el. Lucifer was entertaining a treasonous thought against God's theocracy. He mused, "How wonderful it would be for me to be just like God." In his supernatural intellect became implanted the destructive seed of covetousness. Lucifer was well aware that he should not even consider such vain imaginings. But instead of casting it from his mind it became a seed that would continuously develop, until one day sprouting forth as a mutinous actuality. Lucifer was very much engrossed in his prideful thoughts, when he was snatched back to reality by the thundering voice of the great God Jah-el.

God went on to say, "Let luminaries come to be in the expanse of the heavens to make a division between the day and the night; and they must serve as signs, and for seasons, and for days and for years. They must serve as luminaries in the expanse of the heavens to shine upon the earth." And it came to be so.

The Lord Jah-el proceeded to give His light to the sun and the moon. The sun dominated the day, and the moon dominated the night. This small nine-planet solar system was endowed with an eternal light source that was perfect, and would never burn out. It was a special creation of Jah-el for His world of the corporeal. At the end of His third *creative* day Jah-el had caused vegetation to come forth. Then at the beginning of His fourth *creative* day He spoke light unto the sun, and plant life cloaked the earth flourishing into a global tropical jungle. There was beginning and there came completion, ending this fourth day of Jah-el's creative process on His tiny planet. The angelic servants of God were now in store for an extraordinary surprise!

And God went on to say, "Let the waters of earth become filled with living creatures, and let the flying creatures fly over the surface of the earth, and let them fill the heavens." And God proceeded to create the great whales, the giant mantas, and the like. He created diverse species of fish. The waters teemed with creatures that would reproduce according to their kind, and every flying creature that would reproduce according to its kind. And God saw that it was good. God blessed them saying, "Be fruitful and become many, and fill the earth." And there came to be beginning and there came to be completion, a fifth *creative* day.

Each *creative* day with Jah-el is as a thousand years, and a thousand years as one day. Thus five thousand years had passed in His creation. Five thousand years of His angels intermittently dividing their existence between praising Him, and observing the progression of His visible creation. Jah-el was now about to embark upon the sixth.

These are the generations of the heavens and the earth when they were created, in the days that the Lord Jah-el made Earth and the heavens. The earth gave forth in abundance its vegetation, and there came up a mist from within the earth that watered the ground. It did not rain, for the earth was encapsulated in water. The earth was lush and green. The earth was tropical in all its extent, encased in its global cocoon of water. Toward the third day's ending the Lord God had spoken into existence a variety of greenery. He clothed His earth in cycads, ginkgoes and conifers, amongst them larch, cedar, spruce, hemlock, fir, cypress, juniper, yew, and araucarias. He created ivies and vines, ferns and flowers, in abundance. He created the vegetation in bounty and variety to feed the inhabitants of Earth. He created in proliferation produce-bearing trees and vines laden with edible savory succulent fruits and vegetables.

At the fourth day's onset Jah-el had given light to the sun and the moon. The sun shone through to the earth in a haze. The water canopy that surrounded the earth diffracted the light of the sun, so that it appeared as a great fuzzy orb. It was due to this canopy that the earth's temperature was tropical throughout, for it held the heat from the sun within. The entire earth was beautiful and warm. A perfect place.

On the fifth day Jah-el had spoken into existence all the great wonders of the waters. He had spoken into being all the winged creatures of the air, and they flew within their levels. Within the waters Jah-el had caused to appear three classes of creatures. He had created those amphibious that lived between water and earth. And in proliferation all types of life that lived under the waters, amongst these crustaceans and gill-breathing fish. He created oysters, abalone, clams, lobsters, sea urchins, trilobites, and the like. He created grouper, sea trout, angelfish, salmon, and tuna. He spoke into life sturgeon, pike, and muskellunge. The rays, skates, sharks, squid, octopus, and latimeria were all products of His creative imaginings. The Lord Jah-el filled the waters of His earth with wondrous and amazing creatures as it pleased Him. He caused to come into existence a class of creatures that although air breathers, were bound to Earth's ocean. These were sea-going mammals. The great whales, amongst them the sperms, grays, humpbacks and the enormous blue. These creations were the denizens of the watery deep and navigated the ocean in freedom and peace. Off the shores of the ocean were other manifestations of the handiwork of Jah-el, amongst these were the playful acrobatic porpoises, dolphins, and the awe-inspiring cryptoclieds and plesiosaurs.

Amongst the multifariousness of vegetation dwelt the fowl of the lower levels of the first heaven. The dodo, emu, ostrich, pheasant, peacock, and the like dwelt on or near the earth's floor. The tiny sparrow, wren, hummingbird, finch, and parakeet dwelt in the lower branches of gingkoes and conifers. Great-billed toucans and parrots nested in the upper branches of the towering cycads. The forest was alive with the activity of the fowl of the air. Cockatoos displayed their impressive crests. Birds of paradise darted from branch to branch, their iridescent plumage in tow. Jah-el was well pleased! Along the edges of Earth's rivers and lake shorelines dwelt stilted herons, ibis, and flamingo. Graceful swans glided over the surfaces of still water, as well as many varieties of duck and geese. Along the shores of the ocean dwelt the gulls, terns, sandpipers, and the like. In the high places of the earth dwelt the great condor, and the strangest airborne creatures of all, the quetzals, pterans, and pterads. These were unfeathered flying creatures, with wingspans of up to forty feet. All this Jah-el had accomplished in five *creative* days.

From the time of their creation the creatures of the deep and those of the air had obeyed God's command. They had been fruitful, and they did multiply and fill the earth. Jah-el had created all creatures in pairs, male and female He created them. All higher forms of corporeal animate life stemmed from this union, and they multiplied. He had commanded the creatures of air and water to procreate and fill His earth. Jah-el, in His perfection, would not and could not have the earth overpopulated with any of His creatures. Within them He had implanted a regulator triggered by a law of territory, a law of proximity. In all His fauna would Jah-el implant this governor, for the earth was to be a place of comfort for all that dwelt thereon. When the earth was populated to perfect balance, all procreative activity would cease. As an animal would reach Jah-el's predetermined life span for its species, it would simply expire. It would cease its breath and return to the dust from which it was made. At which point the procreative response in that particular species would become active to fill the void. Because of the earth's perfect environment, the life expectancy of all creatures was long, but only God's crowning creation would have the capacity of eternal life.

In the beginning there was but one ocean. There were no Pacific, Atlantic, Arctic, or Indian oceans. All these oceans of the future in the beginning were occupied by the dry land of one vast continent, the Pangaea. Jah-el had created this vastness of land at the separation of the waters, to assure ample living space for a multitude of offspring from His marvel of marvels.

Everything was according to the plan of the Lord of spirits. In the midst of His reviewing came the beginning of the sixth *creative* day. All that He had accomplished thus far was good in His eyes. And the Lord God continued, saying, "Let the earth bring forth the living creatures after their kind—cattle, reptiles, insects, and all beasts of the earth after their kind." And it was so, and God saw that it was good. He created the cattle, the herding and grazing animals of the field, amongst these the buffalo, antelope, zebra, and the like. He created the reptiles—lizards, crocodiles, alligators, spinos, dimetrodon, ankylos, and the like. He created the serpent. Jah-el produced in profusion countless varieties of insects—cicadas, grasshoppers, termites, beetles, wasps, flies, and bees; ants, worms, foot-long cockroaches, and dragonflies with thirty-inch wingspans. He spoke into existence beautiful multicolored butterflies and moths, a potpourri of buzzing, clicking life.

Of the beasts of the earth Jah-el created the great cats. He created bear, tusk hog, badger, and groundhog. He created the rodents—the opossum, ferret, squirrel, and mice. From the tiny shrew to the magnificent apes, the Lord Jah-el created. In the vast forest of greenery dwelt the elephant. Along the shores of the rivers were the hippopotamuses. All creatures, in Jah-el's perfect order, were primarily herbivores, with the exception of the carrion eaters. From the massive to the miniature it was their duty to accelerate the dust-to-dust cycle. It was Jah-el's natural order for dead flesh to be expediently re-assimilated, but live flesh was not to be eaten, for blood was not to be spilt in pursuance of sustenance. The intentional spilling of blood was taboo, and did not cross the instincts of God's creatures in His perfect order.

The great apes—the gorilla, orangutan, gibbon and chimpanzee—sat perched in fruit laden trees dining on their produce. Beneath the trees discarded pits littered the forest floor, in preparation for continuing its genus of vegetation. Colorful birds of different species diligently pecked apart multi-seed-pocketed pomegranates. Hummingbirds drank from the sweet syrupy nectar of magnolia blossoms, while gigantic pterodactyls glided high overhead. As the vegetation grew in abundance, the animals of the earth fed in abundance, from the smallest insect to the largest sauropod. Jah-el had created an environment that was to be self-sufficient. He had created a planet that in His perfect order would sustain itself forever. He had created a factory of perpetual life, whose existence was based solely on the vegetation of the earth. While Jah-el had created an array of small to moderate-sized creatures, He had also created the earth movers— creatures whose range in size volleyed from the massive to the outrageously colossal. These were the gentle but gigantic gardeners and custodians of the earth. These were the eating machines by which tons of greenery and dead animal flesh would be transformed anew into rich life-propagating fertilizing manure. All animal life had their individual contribution to sustaining mother Earth, but none contributed to her richness as did the ponderous creatures that far into the future would become known as the dinosaur.

These creations were not just merely overgrown lizards, but an integral and important element of Jah-el's creation. These creatures were unique not only as to type, but also in appearance and purpose. They were the most fascinating of the land rovers; different, a category of beast all to themselves. Amongst these Jah-el created the sauropods— camaras, brontos, alamos, diplidocus, laplats, branchios, haplocanthos, memenchis, and the like. These were great beasts that dwelt in herds. With long sweeping ostrich-like necks, lizard-like tails, small heads, and massive bodies, they would walk the earth on all fours, their tonnage sending shock waves as their huge elephant-like feet pounded the ground. Ranging in lengths of fifteen to eighty-five feet, and weighting from one to forty tons, these creatures would both clear and browse mature forest. They could eat the leaves, nuts, and fruit of trees as far up as thirty-five feet. Or they could wade belly deep into rivers and lakes and scoop up great mouthfuls of aquatic vegetation off the bottom. Their fecal matter in water would provide the aquatic life with an abundance of partially digested sustenance. On land this same waste matter would provide great deposits of manure, from which undigested seeds would spring to new life. Browsing steadily from river and forest alike, these creatures would convert a prodigious mass of vegetation into rich fertilizer. With the movement of such creatures they would transport a wealth of this life-motivating commodity from one range to the next, replenishing the earth. This was the chief duty of these great beasts of the earth, to give renewed richness to the soil from which would grow new generations of vegetation.

The Lord God Jah-el spoke into existence in this sixth *creative* day the ornithopods—iguanodons, pachycelphalos, othnielis, sceidos, callovos, heterodonotos, tanontos, fabros, psittacos, allos, tyranos, meglos, albertas, demonychus, alloramus, phobosochus, and the like. These were they that walked on two legs, having also stunted fore legs with small talon like claws. These ranged in height three to forty feet, and weighed ten pounds to eight tons.

Jah-el created the genus Ceratopsian with their elaborate bony frills that covered much of their necks, back, and tails. These were also endowed with horns, much like those of the rhinoceros. He created the genus Hadros, and that of Stegos. The Lord Jah-el had created them also in pairs, and all the beasts of the earth lived in His harmony, and in one accord.

The Lord God planted a garden eastward, called Eden. In this garden, out of its ground, Jah-el caused to grow every tree that is pleasant to the sight and good for food. In the middle of this garden Jah-el planted two special trees. One was called the tree of life. This tree is a very fragrant tree.

Its aroma is beyond that of any vegetation that the Lord God created. Its leaves, blossoms, and wood are eternal, and never wither. Its fruit is beautiful, glowing, and resembles the date of palms. The second tree that Jah-el planted was the tree of the knowledge of good and evil. This tree is in height like the fir, its leaves like those of the carob tree, its fruit like the clusters of the vine; exquisite, and its fragrance penetrates afar.

There was a river issuing out of Eden to water the garden, and from this place of origin it parted and became four heads. The first river's name is Pison, and encircles the entire land of Hav'ilah, where there is gold, bdellium, and the onyx stone. The name of the second river is Gi'hon. The third river is the river Tigris, which runs toward the east of Assyria, and the fourth is the river Euphrates.

It was now the twilight of His sixth *creative* day. Jah-el sat upon His throne, and from the time of the planting of Eden, was once again mysteriously silent. For a space of time His creative activity had ceased. His power had ceased to surge. His angels sensed, that from the walled creation of Eden, something stupendous was about to transpire! All eyes in the third heaven were fixed upon the blinding presence occupying the throne chariot.

Michael, Gabriel, Raphael, and Uriel stood transfixed at their corner posts, awaiting what Jah-el would decree next. Lucifer stood fascinated in his inner sanctum position, attempting to anticipate just what Jah-el would purpose next. Suddenly, without warning or explanation, Jah-el spoke a baffling command to Lucifer. He said to His magnificent cherub, "Lucifer I have in mind an added duty for you. It is My decree that you and all the angels under your command should go to My new creation, Earth. I am about to place within the walls of the garden My marvel of marvels, and when I do I shall send Michael with further instruction to you. Go now to the area that is the fountain-head of the four rivers. Go to the place called Eden."

Lucifer was perplexed and somewhat incensed. Why should he have to leave his position from the left hand side of God? After all, he was Lucifer the beautiful, the bright and morning star. Why should he have to leave the third heaven, travel through finite space, and station himself in the first heaven surrounding this tiny planet Earth? True it was a special planet, but it was so far beneath him. It was so far beneath Jah-el and His seat of authority. Why him? Why not Michael, who was less beautiful than he?

Lucifer lifted himself aloft on his great golden wings. He summoned all that were placed under his command. He and his brethren flew through the throne room of God, through the great vestibule, and through the portal of the third heaven that separates the spirit and finite realms. Lucifer traveled through space at reckless velocity, his brethren finding it difficult to keep up with him. "If I am to be ordered below my status, then I shall not obey such commands. I will—" Lucifer caught himself. These thoughts were dangerous. After all, these thoughts were contrary to the will of God. Lucifer had discovered himself. He had discovered his will, and it was completely opposite to the will of Jah-el. Little did Lucifer realize that Jah-el was not only all-powerful, but all-knowing as well. His deviant thoughts were not as private as he believed. Jah-el in His triuneness had spoken concerning him prior to his being created. He was soon to become that spirit creature who would cause chaos amongst all that Jah-el had created. Lucifer and his command reached their destination, entered through the earth's water canopy, and placed themselves above Eden. They with supernatural sight perused the landscape and all that Jah-el had placed in this corporeal existence.

Michael, Gabriel, Raphael, Uriel, and all the angelic hosts of God stationed on the sea of glass below heard Jah-el decree in a mighty voice of thunder, "Let Us make man in Our image, according to Our likeness, and let them have in subjection the fish of the sea, the flying creatures of the heavens, and the beasts of the earth, and everything that moves upon the surface of the earth." The angels of heaven were puzzled. Why did the great Jah-el speak in the plural, for throughout all creation He had not been inclusive before. Was He speaking of them? What could be the meaning of this? Jah-el proceeded to create man, His marvel of marvels, in His own image. Jah-el proceeded to form man out of the dust of the ground and to blow into his nostrils the breath of life, and man came to be a living soul. Jah-el created His marvel of marvels, a spirit being encased inside a shell of flesh, and called his name Adam. Lucifer and his command were overwhelmed by this surprise! To be in the presence of Jah-el when He spoke into being was one thing, but to watch creation appear without introduction was somewhat disconcerting.

Lucifer found this creature unnerving, as he was overcome by an inexplicable sense of threat. "What is this creature that Jah-el has formed? How does it fit into His plan?" Lucifer pondered uncomfortably. "Whatever this earth creature is, it is certainly different from all others. There is something unique about this creation," he mused. He didn't know how or why, but there was something about this new creation that most assuredly disturbed him.

The angels in heaven upon seeing Adam rejoiced greatly. They were astonished by this marvel of marvels.

Here was a creature: corporeal, intelligent, perfect, and made in the image of God, a tangible reflection of the Most High God Himself. Jah-el took the man Adam and settled him into the Garden. He told Adam this was his home, and that he was to cultivate and take care of it. And the Lord God commanded the man saying, "Of every tree of this garden you may eat to your satisfaction, but of the tree of the knowledge of good and evil you must not eat; for in the day that you eat of it, you will positively die."

Out of the ground Jah-el formed every living thing on Earth. And over time He brought them all before Adam, to see what Adam would call them. Adam gave names to every living thing that crept upon the earth. God created each species male and female that they might procreate. Jah-el had created in pairs. It was now time for Him to create the help-mate of his crowning creation.

The Lord caused a deep sleep to fall upon Adam. While Adam slumbered, God the Father gave the command by God the Son, and the Holy Spirit opened Adam's side and took from him a rib. And Jah-el proceeded to build around that rib which He had taken, a woman. From the dust of the ground Jah-el created Adam, but from the rib of man did He create woman. God caused Adam to rise from his deep sleep, and brought to him his woman. Upon seeing her Adam cried out in adoring joy, "This is at last bone of my bone, and flesh of my flesh. This one shall be called woman, because from me was she taken. She shall be called Eve." They were both naked, the man and his wife, but there was no shame. All was perfect, and the way that Jah-el had planned. Jah-el blessed them and said to them, "Be fruitful, and multiply, and fill the earth and subdue it. Have in subjection every living creature that is upon the face of the earth, whether in the heavens above, or in the waters below.

I have provided for you all vegetation and fruit-bearing trees upon the surface of the earth, that it may serve you as food. To the lower forms of life that inhabit your earth, I give them the green vegetation for food." It was the duty of the man to see to it that his wife learned the statute of limitation that Jah-el had placed upon the tree of knowledge. Adam fulfilled his duty, and told Eve all concerning this.

Lucifer had been deprived of the third heaven through all of the time it had taken from man's creation till this point. It was clearly obvious to his command that by now Lucifer had become strangely uneasy. Lucifer seethed as he and his command hid behind their cloaks of invisibility, but he kept his discontent silent. He knew that the reasoning behind his being at this place was somehow connected to this new creation, but how? All that Jah-el had decreed had come to be, and He looked upon it from His throne and saw that it was good. The completion was now setting upon this sixth day of creation, the stilling of all the works of His hands, and the beginning of the new day brought one that was like no other. The heavens and the earth were at their completion, and all that was to be therein. This new beginning brought forth the seventh day.

God blessed this seventh day and sanctified it. It was designated a sacred day because on this day Jah-el was now at rest. The period of creation was finished, issuing forth what was to be an eternity of bliss. The intensity of Jah-el the creator was concluded. He called to Himself Michael, and the other corner cherubim. Upon their gathering around His throne the Lord God spoke and said, "Michael, call forth your brethren from the sea of glass below which are like unto yourself, and also all of the seraphim. Have them station themselves in my presence that I may speak to them." Michael did as Jah-el commanded. The twenty-four-winged cherubim and the seraphim took their places respectively, while the ophanim and the sixteen-winged cherubim remained stationed on the sea of glass below. When all were in order, Jah-el issued a new decree. God demanded saying, "Behold the man Adam, the marvel of marvels, he that is My crowning creation. He alone is created in My image. You shall therefore be his servants also, to minister unto his needs. You will watch over them, the man Adam and his wife. It is My decree that you serve the man who is created in My image, but never is he to serve you. For I am the Lord God Jah-el, and I have spoken." The angelic hordes of God began praising the Most High. They bowed low before Jah-el in worship, and before His image Adam in semblance of their servitude. Michael was the first in obedience of His Lord God's command.

In the midst of the celebration in the third heaven, the dominion of Jah-el, the Lord God called Michael to Himself. Jah-el gave Michael, His angel of might, a special assignment. He said, "Michael, go by way of the portal that separates spirit and finite. Travel the distance of the second division of heaven to the first, and deliver this instruction to Lucifer your brother. Tell him that I have decided him Chief Watcher over paradise, he and all his command. Tell him that he is to be chief guardian of the man Adam and his wife. Tell him that he is to serve them as he would serve Me, for the man Adam is created in My image. Tell him it is My will that both he and his command bow before, and serve the marvel of marvels, My crowning creation—Man." Michael sped away from before the throne of God, across the sea of glass, through the massive vestibule, through the portal of the third heaven and into the finite world. Michael flashed through the space of the second division of heaven, spanning the cosmos as only a cherub of his order can. He arrived to find his brother Lucifer and his command watching the human pair from behind their cloak of invisibility.

Michael's arrival caught Lucifer completely by surprise. Michael confronted the startled Lucifer, the magnificent angel of light, "Lucifer my brother, this is what the Lord Jah-el has decreed for you. You are to be the servant, you and your command of our brethren, to the man Adam. He is the image of Jah-el Himself, and you are to minister unto him and his wife. Now bow before the image of God in semblance to your acceptance of Jah-el's decree. It is the will of God." Lucifer convulsed in anger. His pride rose up and erupted from his mouth and he blared, "I am Lucifer, the bright and morning star. I am he that is created most beautiful amongst all angelic creatures. My place is in the third heaven, beside the throne of Jah-el!" Michael interjected, "Be careful my brother Lucifer. For your place is wherever our Creator decrees it to be. Be careful that you not test Him." Lucifer's vexation had now catapulted into vehement rage and he sneered, "I have no need to subjugate myself to Adam. Why do you entreat me to serve this inferior creation? I will not serve him, for he is a younger creation than myself! I am his senior in creation! Before he was made was I already made. It is his obligation to bow before me!" Michael immediately rebuked Lucifer saying, "Be careful in what you say Lucifer, for Jah-el has spoken from His seat of authority that we are to be servant unto man, but never is he to be servant unto us. Be careful that you not test our God."

Still Lucifer remained adamant. In self-righteous indignation he retorted, "I will not serve this creature Adam or his wife. I care not that Jah-el may find displeasure with me. If Jah-el will be angry with me then I shall ascend into heaven, and I will exalt my throne above the stars of God. I will sit upon the mount of the congregation in the sides of the north. I will ascend above the heights, and I will be like the Most High." Michael, upon hearing this, recognized the madness of his brother Lucifer. The angels that were under Lucifer's command, upon hearing the declaration of their leader, also refused to obey the order of Jah-el. Michael stood in stunned disbelief at the insanity of Lucifer and his followers. Before he embarked on his journey home, Michael, saddened by the choice of Lucifer and his band, said in remorse, "Lucifer, my brother of great beauty, your vestige is your downfall. Your fate is surely sealed, and your doom shortly to follow. I go now to make known your error before His throne."

Michael returned before the Lord Jah-el and relayed to Him all that had occurred on Earth. The angels of the third heaven quaked in great fear for their brother Lucifer and his following. How could he sin against the decree of Jah-el Himself? What could he possibly gain? Could the created overthrow the Creator? What would Jah-el do to Lucifer, and what fate belied their angelic brethren for also choosing to disregard His edict? These and countless other questions plagued the supernatural intellects of the angelic hosts of God. Jah-el dismissed Michael from before His presence with this instruction, "When you see Lucifer coming through the great vestibule return you, Gabriel, Raphael, and Uriel to me. Allow Lucifer and his cohorts audience before Me, for I have commanded them hither by My own voice."

Lucifer soon arrived through the great opening between the vestibule and throne room of God, his command of angels trailing behind. Michael, upon seeing them gave the order. The shield wings of he and the other three covering cherubim shot into place. They moved into their audience positions in closer proximity to God. Jah-el peered forward and observed Lucifer boldly coming toward Him, his golden wings shimmering. What gall this creature had, to disobey Him and then come unrepentant before His throne. Jah-el was incensed. He knew that before Him was approaching the beginning of chaos. He would deal with this creature in a way that would completely disavow his rantings as gross error. He would allow Lucifer the opportunity to prove his boastings, before inflicting final judgment upon him. With Lucifer proven impotent in his ability to be just like Himself, Jah-el would never again tolerate such a creature whether in the spirit or corporeal realms. So that there would be no doubts amongst His angelic hosts as to whether Lucifer could make good his threats, Jah-el would allow Lucifer a modicum of time. The throne room of God was mute. Not one of the angels of heaven uttered a sound, as Lucifer set himself down before God. Jah-el thundered in a measured demand, "Lucifer, what is this that you have refused My command?"

Lucifer remained silent, thinking that his insolent entrance had already brought Jah-el to the brink of speaking upon him instant retribution. Jah-el thundered anew, this time less reserved, "Lucifer thou wicked and unappreciative cherub, what is this that you have refused to obey My command?" Lucifer, sensing no endearing, forgiving, or empathetic tone in the voice of Jah-el, was bolstered to renewed obstinacy. This was his point of no return, and so Lucifer lifted his head in arrogance and replied, "Jah-el, there is no reason that I should recount to You all that I have said. I am sure that Michael has reported all that took place in the vicinity of the garden on your planet Earth. I am Lucifer, the bright and morning star. It is beneath me to serve that inferior being that You call man. I will not obey Your order, nor will my angels with me."

Jah-el's voice was extremely calm as He spoke rebuttal to the treasonous cherub. Jah-el responded, "Lucifer, you have taken a great task upon yourself. You have purposed yourself to be just as I am. If we are equals, then before this congregation take down your shield wings and let us speak face to face." Lucifer shuddered at the thought, bringing a redefined perspective to his present situation. He could not look directly into the face of God. Jah-el was humiliating him, diminishing his stature in the presence of his fellow angels. In seconds that seemed to Lucifer like eons, he intimately queried Jah-el's toleration of his rebelliousness as to what would happen to him and his angelic command. He did not have to wait much longer for the decree of punishment from the great God Jah-el.

Jah-el reared back in His seat of power, pointing an accusatory finger toward Lucifer and proclaimed,

"You have decreed that My command means nothing to you, and that My wrath towards you is unimportant. You have vowed in your vanity to ascend into My heaven, and exalt your throne above your brethren. You have vowed to establish yourself upon the mount of the congregation in the sides of the north. You have vowed to raise yourself above the heights, and to become just like Me. How foolish you are O Lucifer. You have brought to an end your pattern of wisdom. Your beauty is blemished, and your glory is brought to an end. You were once holy, but now you are stripped of your holiness. In My Garden of Eden I commissioned you to be. I created you more magnificent than all your brethren. You were the anointed cherub of covering. You were mine to appoint as it pleased Me. In the midst of your brethren you went about in your great beauty. I admonished you from your beginning to be not wise in thine own wisdom O Lucifer, and to be not taken with thy excellent grandeur. You were once faultless in all your ways, until this unrighteousness was found in you. You have done a deed unprecedented. You have caused chaos and doubt amongst your brethren concerning Me. For this will I cast you as profane from before My presence, and I shall remove you from the midst of your brethren. Your demeanor became haughty due to thy beauty. You brought your wisdom to ruin because of thy beaming splendor. Onto the earth I will cast you, Lucifer. I shall make you ashes upon the earth, before the eyes of all who look upon you. You are banished from your permanent residency here O Lucifer, but I shall tolerate your audience before Me until I decree it to be no longer. You are banished to live in the finite and corporeal heaven, outside My heaven. My plan and My purpose were set long before you and your brethren were created. It was set when I was alone, and there was nothing. My word does not and will never return unto Me void. I am granting you a segment of time O Lucifer, to make good your idle threats. I am granting to you a period of time to bring to rest any doubt amongst your brethren, that you might be able to carry out your vile rantings. Then Lucifer, upon your failure shall you be abyssed throughout all eternity from before their faces."

Jah-el commanded Michael to take hold of Lucifer. Gabriel, Raphael, Uriel, and a multitude of faithful angels were commanded by Jah-el to take hold of all their brethren that had followed Lucifer. Jah-el demanded, "Remove these your fallen brethren to the portals of the third heaven, and cast them out into the finite world. Station guardians at the mouth of the portals that they may never again, enter into this realm. These are banished forever, except for their leader Lucifer."

Adam and Eve were unaware of the beginning of sin and chaos in the third heaven. They were unaware that an angel named Lucifer was in the vicinity of them when he had refused an order from Jah-el. Adam did not realize that at that moment, Lucifer and a third of the stars of heaven were being cast out into the finite world. He was oblivious to the fact that soon his wife would be confronted, by this very angel. There was nothing to be concerned about, for Adam personally knew and was spoken to directly by Jah-el. The only wrong that either could possibly do, was eat of the forbidden tree. He would never do such a thing. After all, Jah-el had warned against this infraction with His own voice; and besides, Adam knew that in the day he ate of this tree he would positively die.

Lucifer and his command had made themselves outcasts. They had erroneously exercised their freedom of choice. It was their prerogative to do so, but at the cost of forfeiting their holiness. They were now profane, abased, and Jah-el could no longer tolerate their presence in His holy realm. They had become the fallen stars, the sons of darkness. Lucifer's sin was self-contained. He had not gone out of his way to persuade any of his command to follow his insubordination. Jah-el had spoken the order to His arch-cherub Michael. Michael relayed that order. Lucifer's command of the angelic servants of God had willfully chosen to follow him in disobedience. It was not out of any great love for this fallen cherub that Jah-el had not imprisoned him into oblivion, but out of justice. Lucifer's punishment would befit his crime. He had disobeyed his Commander in Chief, and was therefore judged, stripped of his rank, and dishonorably discharged from the kingdom of Jah-el.

Lucifer hovered, fixed upon nothing, in the cold vacuum of finite space, he and his angels with him. His hatred blazed. He hated Jah-el for what he had come to perceive as His slight to his former position, but above all he hated that image-creation Adam. Lucifer had quickly become the most demented force in the cosmos. He was outraged! His screams of vengeance echoed throughout the finite chasm of the second heaven. He made a vow within to destroy all that was the perfect order of Jah-el. He hovered, his eyes fixed upon the now-guarded portals of the third heaven. The cherubim of the guard wielding the swords of the Spirit that turned continuously, blocking entrance. The third of the stars of heaven that fell with Lucifer were not as belligerent as he. They found themselves in exceedingly great discomfort and turmoil. They would never be allowed home again. They were banished forever!

Lucifer whirled to face them, testily re-asserting his dominance by ridiculing their fear. "We are not conquered," he bellowed. "This is but our beginning! I will prove to Jah-el that I am not to be classified a small matter. I am Lucifer, the bright and morning star!" Lucifer rallied his forces, and gave his first unholy command as dark lord. They were once again to return to the vicinity of Earth. Just outside Earth's atmosphere, at the top of its northern pole, Lucifer placed his invisible kingdom and seat of authority. Lucifer was proving to be a charismatic leader, and soon soothed the disquiet of his army. He said to Semjazael and Azazel, two of his generals, "We have become a power within ourselves. I have set myself in opposition to everything that is Jah-el. I shall convince Him that Lucifer is a force to be reckoned with. I, and all my angels with me. I have in mind to cause Jah-el great pain and grief, and it shall be wrought through that disgusting creature He calls man."

CHAPTER 3

THE FALL OF CREATION

Heaven was not ignorant of the schemes of Lucifer. Jah-el was well aware of the coming attack directed toward His son Adam. It was for this reason that He had given Adam the command concerning the tree of the knowledge of good and evil. Not only was Jah-el aware, He was also cognizant of the outcome. This scheme of Lucifer's would soon prove to his detriment, providing Jah-el ample justification to condemning him to eternal imprisonment. Jah-el had given both to His angelic creation and His image-creation, the freedom of choice. He had not created them robots, but free moral agents. Like Lucifer, Adam's destiny was a matter of decision. No one had coerced Lucifer to rebel; it was solely his choice. Choice—the word that would soon come to mean eternal delight or eternal damnation to all mankind. It was this six-letter word that would soon cost Lucifer his freedom.

The four rivers whose origin was from Paradise each ran their own course, watering the Garden planted by God Himself. Rainbow and golden trout, iridescent bluegill and silvery Minnows, propelled themselves amongst the tall rushes that swayed back and forth in a gentle breeze. Dragonflies darted about, skimming the surface of still water in their nervous style. The fragrances of countless varieties of flowers intermingled with the heavenly aroma of the tree of the knowledge of good and evil. Adam and his wife wandered past it, without even stopping to consider it. This tree was the sole property of Jah-el; He had given them every tree of the Garden for food, it was not necessary for them to have this one also.

Butterflies flittered across the open meadow, which was a virtual sea of clover and multi-colored morning glories. Bees buzzed about, lending the humming of their wings to the symphony of chirpings from gaily colored song birds and the continuous din of cicadas. Nearby, on one of the lakes birthed by the excess of waters from the four rivers, swam alabaster white and indigo black swans. Mallards and geese intermingled in harmony upon the surface, tending their young. Stilted whooping cranes and flamingos waded amongst its water lilies. In the shallows a tree had fallen; it was alive with salamanders and newts. A painted turtle at its upper end dropped lazily into the water, just prior to Adam and Eve's arrival.

Adam and his wife stood a little ways off from the fallen tree, enjoying the breathtaking panorama of the Garden of Eden. In the near distance was a great forest of pine trees, their pointed tops steepled toward heaven. They stood as tall dark green silhouettes against the aquamarine sky. Small rolling hills could be seen just to the left, jutting from the earth like camel humps. Along the shoreline were creatures of all sorts, wading and drinking. Near the bullrushes amid a sprinkling of partially submerged boulders peeked the face of a lone crocodile, eyes periscoped from just below the surface.

Adam took his wife's hand and they continued their stroll about their home. They passed a family of lambeos sitting upon their haunches; with their smaller forelegs bracing against a pear tree they picked its fruit. How beautiful they were with their umber bodies, viridian stripes, and bony head crests.

The Garden was host to some of the more massive beasts that Jah-el had created. There were hippopotamuses, elephants, and rhinoceroses. There were ceratopsians, stegos, a few species from the genus Ornithopod and Hadros. The more massive and colossal beasts such as the sauropods, and the larger ornithopods Jah-el caused to be outside of the Garden. Jah-el had said to Adam that he should be fruitful, multiply, and populate the earth with humankind. Jah-el had also informed Adam to enlarge the garden condition of Eden to encompass the entire Pangaea. In time it would be so, but in the meanwhile Jah-el had prepared well for the earth. Adam and Eve would cultivate the land inside the Garden, and the gigantic sauropods and the like would do so outside. As man would multiply and cover the face of the earth, these gigantic creatures would cease to exist. It was the will of Jah-el. He had placed within them a procreative regulator, triggered by territorial stress. This regulator would act upon the birth process of these huge beasts. The closer man in their proximity, the more the waning of their procreation. As man covered the face of the globe, these great beasts would eventually and peacefully die out.

All animals died. Only man had the capacity of everlasting life. Its retention rested solely on his choice to obey the mandate of Jah-el. Jah-el had decreed, "Of every tree of this Garden you may eat to your satisfaction, but of the tree of the knowledge of good and evil you must not eat. For in the day that you eat, you will positively die." Adam and his wife knew the meaning of death. They had seen animals die. In one moment they were and in the next moment they were not; lifeless, only a shell remaining. How perplexing and shrouded in mystery was this thing called death.

Eve stopped to cuddle a newborn fawn. She stooped, and the infant licked her face and hands. Adam stood alongside the buck and doe, feeding them a clutch of tender grass. All of the animals of the earth loved Adam and his wife, and they them. Eve stood, turned, and embraced her husband. She was happy, and together they shared the joy given them by God. They continued on their way, toward a path that would lead them to one of their favorite spots in their Garden home.

The first human pair walked naked, and without shame, being at peace with their Creator and their surroundings. They moved away from the lake and pursued one of its tributaries upstream. They walked beneath the fan-leafed gingkoes that grew in abundance. The sun hazed through their leaves like a great fuzzy orb. They approached a favorite haunt. Just ahead of this racing brook, which coursed over smooth granite rocks, was a large clear pool. Here the deer, springbuck, and zebra came to sip the refreshing water. Families of serpentine-trunked elephants stripped succulent leaves from overhanging trees. There were large boulders strewn along the perimeter of the pool, upholstered in yellowish green lichen. Upon these were perched fin-backed dimetrodons, and white egrets in proliferation. Wading in the pool a lone stegos refreshed itself. Playful monkeys swung about overhead, and the birds of paradise nested in the conglomeration of moss-laden trees. There were parrots of every hue, great beaked macaws, and crested cockatoo. Peacock strutted their bright plumage. The songbirds performed their acrobatics as they winged from branch to branch. Adam and Eve frolicked, smiled, and laughed together. They praised Jah-el, for they knew He was worthy of praise.

Jah-el had provided food in fantastic array. At arms' length there were bananas, peaches, dates, grapes, and figs. There were melons of every variety in the open fields. There were apples, plums, every sort of citrus fruit, and more, much more. A tiger panted lazily as he lay beneath the shade of a spreading schefflera, taking occasional glimpses at the activities going on about him. There was life everywhere, and all things operated within the perfect order of Jah-el.

The angels of the Most High ministered to Adam and his wife. They appeared to them, and brought messages from their God. At times Jah-el would speak to Adam directly. Adam was perfect, holy, and unblemished before Jah-el. With their heads held erect, Adam and his wife worshipped and praised the Lord of spirits. They proclaimed, "You are the only wise and true Creator Jah-el, and we are your children. Find favor with us always, for we are truly in paradise."

As they praised the name of Jah-el, the birds of heaven sang praises with Eve. The beasts of the field surrounded Adam and reclined, manifesting their subjection. Jah-el had created man in His own image, and he was master of his home Earth.

Of all the beasts that roamed the face of earth, the serpent proved to be the most subtle. It was an intriguing creation with its long slender body, and with small curled claws affixed to short scampering legs it was adept to climbing. It had on its back two folds of skin, that when stretched out enabled it to glide from tree to tree. Not only that, but like some of Jah-el's creations of the heavens, the serpent could talk. It was capable of mimicry. Jah-el had provided it two tiny but keenly sensitive ears that stood atop its triangular head like little horns. It was a shy and elusive creature, and would scurry and hide whenever anyone or anything would approach. Serpents fascinated Adam and Eve, but especially Eve. As the serpents learned more and more of the human language, they could be heard throughout the Garden repeating all that they learned. This brought Eve tremendous joy. "What clever little creatures," she mused. She would spend hours beneath a tree in which a serpent dwelt, her beaming face tilted upward, pleading in her most coaxing feminine voice, "Come down little serpent, come down and show yourself. There is no need for you to hide. Come down that I may teach you many wonderful things to say."

Lucifer sat restlessly on the throne he had prepared for himself atop the northern pole of the earth, just outside its atmosphere. From there he observed the activities of the human pair. He watched Adam and Eve as they carried out the decrees of Jah-el. He watched the comings and goings of his brethren, the angelic servants of Jah-el, as they ministered to Adam and Eve. Lucifer sat upon his dark throne, in his dominion of gloom, contemplating his revenge.

Suddenly, added wickedness arose in the heart of the fallen cherub. He summoned one from amongst his ranks, an angel named Gadreel. Lucifer said to Gadreel, "I have come upon a plan, one to cause great grief and discomfort to Jah-el. I shall lead astray the man that is called Adam. I shall accomplish it through his wife Eve, by means of the serpent which she adores so much." Gadreel mused over the statement of his dark lord for a moment, then inquired of him in bewilderment, "How shall you accomplish this scheme lord Lucifer, and how is the serpent involved?" Lucifer became possessed of sinister joy, as he roared forth great peals of diabolical laughter. Lucifer boomed forth the name of his comrade Gadreel saying, "Through the serpent I shall deceive Eve, and through her I shall cause the fall of that creature Adam. I shall become master of the earth and all therein. This is what we shall do Gadreel. When the angels of Jah-el have departed, and returned to the third heaven to worship before His throne, I shall appear unto Eve and convince her to eat of the tree of the knowledge of good and evil. When I appear before her disguised as an angel of light, you Gadreel shall maneuver into place the elusive serpent. Come closer Gadreel and heed my command as to what you are to do."

Tomorrow was the seventh day. Jah-el had decreed that since the demise of Lucifer, no holy angel in the vicinity of the earth could stay beyond six *earth* days. On the sixth day the holy angels on earth must return to the third heaven to worship before the throne of Jah-el. It had come such a time for Uriel and Saraqael. They bade Adam a fond farewell until their return, then they lifted themselves on their magnificent wings and ascended into heaven.

Adam once again set himself to the work prescribed him by Jah-el. The Garden of Eden was being transformed by the creative whims of its occupants. Adam reflected over the words of Jah-el delivered to him by Uriel and Saraqael, especially their repeated admonishments of total obedience to the Ancient of Days. As Adam carried out his work in the northeast segment of the Garden, Eve was walking about in the southwest portion near the wall surrounding the Garden. Here Eve was intrigued by a small flock of female animals, feeding them the vegetation of the earth from her hands.

Lucifer and Gadreel arrived in the Garden of Eden. After making certain that Adam and Eve were apart Lucifer commissioned Gadreel to seek out a serpent, and after possessing that serpent to meet him in the southwest segment of the Garden by the wall where Eve was. Gadreel went forth and did as his dark lord commanded. He found a serpent and prior to entering him said, "Rise up, come that you may serve the purpose of Lucifer. You are the most cautious and wise of all beasts. You are to be the vessel of Lucifer and through you shall he speak words to deceive the woman Eve, for you are a special creation of Jah-el and she will believe you." Gadreel entered the serpent and immediately caused it to go to the place foreordained by Lucifer.

As Eve continued in her leisure, she became aware she was not alone. She heard singing, singing like that of the angels of Jah-el. She stood still, attentive, attempting to locate the direction from which this sweet voice was coming. The animals that surrounded her bolted in all directions. "What a strange way for them to act," she thought. The hymn of praise was now being sung at a higher decibel. She knew the direction from which it came. It was coming from near the wall about thirty feet away, behind a cluster of hedges and willow trees.

As Eve approached, to her amazement she was met by a sight of intense beauty. She had seen the angels of Jah-el before, but none like this one. As she stepped forth into the clearing Lucifer cooed, "Are you Eve?" Eve answered in a state of mesmerization, "Yes, I am Eve." Lucifer moved closer. He glided forth as if lifted by a gentle breeze, rested his great golden wings, and with his face like unto a man continued to question her saying, "What are you doing here in Paradise?" Eve responded, "The Lord God Jah-el has made us and set us over the Garden that we may cultivate it, and eat of its produce. That we may multiply and become many and extend this garden over the entire earth, for He has given it as our home."

Lucifer had Eve exactly where he wanted her. He had successfully engaged her; now he would put into effect the trump of his malicious plan. He would question her even further but not by his own mouth, but with the mouth of her favorite creature the elusive serpent.

Gadreel within the serpent had set it in the exact location predetermined by Lucifer. The serpent sat clutched to the wall in an upside down position peering out at Eve. With all the skill of a perfect ventriloquist, Lucifer threw his voice into the serpent saying, "You are provided for well, but you do not eat of every tree that is in your garden?" Eve spun in total amazement toward the direction from which this new voice emerged. She could not believe her eyes. There before her was a serpent, the evasive and vastly fascinating little creature she had so often pursued. Here was one before her, talking to her. Eve had taken her eyes away from Lucifer, and fixed them firmly upon the serpent. She naively answered, "We eat of all the trees of this garden save for one only, which is the tree that is located in the middle of the garden, which is the tree of the knowledge of good and evil. It is the tree that is exclusively the property of the Lord Jah-el. He has said we must not eat from it, nor even touch it, for in the day that we eat thereof we will positively die." The serpent spread its glide wings and sprang from the wall of Paradise onto a low branch of a young sycamore. Eve was spellbound. She completely forgot about Lucifer, and cast her full attention on the serpent. The serpent purred back sage-like, "May God live, but on your account am I sadly grieved; therefore, I shall not have you ignorant. Come closer, listen to me, and I shall tell you of the value of the tree that you may eat of it." Eve recoiled in shock. "I cannot eat of the tree that is Jah-el's, for fear that He will be displeased with me." The serpent left its perch and presented itself on the ground, standing before Eve, gazing up at her with its tiny eyes, and said to her in a tone of unequivocal assurance, "Fear not Eve for as soon as you eat of the tree you shall be just like Jah-el Himself, in that you shall know the difference between good and evil. The reason that Jah-el has commanded you not to eat of the tree is because He does not want you to be like Himself. His motive is entirely selfish. Do not be afraid, follow me to the tree and I shall give you of its fruit." Eve opened to the suggestion of the serpent; it made sense. "Why shouldn't I be like God?" she thought.

The serpent scampered ahead of Eve, leading her to the tree in the middle of the Garden. Eve was now addicted to this idea of the serpent's. He had deceived her into placing her will above that of Jah-el's. Eve saw the serpent, but what she did not see was the evil and invisible force behind the serpent. She had totally dismissed the presence of Lucifer. Lucifer was ecstatic in his vileness. He had pulled the perfect switch. Eve was about to become his implement against Adam. So far his plan was working.

Without warning, the serpent stopped dead in its tracks. It turned and said to Eve, "I have changed my mind. I will not give you to eat of the tree until you swear unto me an oath, that you will give the fruit also to your husband Adam." By this time the thought of being like Jah-el was embedded firmly in the heart of Eve. She stammered to the serpent, "What sort of oath shall I swear?" She grasped at all that she considered sacred, save the name of Jah-el, and formed them into an oath, saying to the serpent, "By the throne of the Master, and by the cherubim of the tree of life, I vow to give to my husband Adam also from the forbidden tree." With that the serpent continued to the tree of the knowledge of good and evil. It climbed into it, found a low-hanging branch, and bent it down so Eve could grab a cluster. Lucifer, through the serpent, poured upon the fruit the poison of his wickedness, which is lust, the root and beginning of every sin. Eve, intoxicated with her wantonness, plucked and ate the forbidden fruit.

At the instance she ate of the fruit her eyes were opened. She was stripped of the innocence of her perfection, and knew she was naked. Eve wept bitterly, hurling accusation at the serpent pleading, "Why have you done this evil thing to me, depriving me of the glory in which I was once clothed?" The serpent did not answer, but disappeared into the low-lying brush. With its work completed, Lucifer released the serpent. Eve was now frantic; she was naked, she must cover up! At the moment she had partaken of the forbidden fruit, the fruit and blossoms of the trees surrounding her fell rotted to the ground; from the leaves of a fig tree she fashioned a covering.

Eve gathered the remainder of the cluster of fruit, remembering her oath, and set out to find her husband Adam. She began calling out to him, "Adam, Adam, where are you?" Upon finally hearing her voice Adam answered, "Here I am." Eve continued saying, "Adam! Stop whatever you are doing, and come to me that I might show you a great secret." When Adam arrived, she opened her mouth and the voice of Lucifer proceeded from her lips. Eve said, "Come closer to me my lord Adam. Listen to me, and eat of this the fruit from the forbidden tree of Jah-el. For at the moment you eat of it you shall be just like Jah-el Himself, knowing the difference between good and evil." Adam recoiled, "I fear to do such a thing Eve, lest Jah-el be displeased with me." Eve placed the forbidden fruit in her husband's hand coaxing, "Fear not."

In the instant Adam ate of the forbidden fruit, his eyes too were opened. But something even more devastating occurred. Creation fell. The flowers and fruit of every variety of vegetation throughout the entire Pangaea, save the two trees of Jah-el, dropped rotted to the ground. The living creatures of the earth were thrown into instant confusion. From the tiny ant to the gigantic sauropods, creation was in chaos. Sweet-throated songbirds began to screech. Elephants began to trumpet. Lions began to roar. The herds began to stampede. The earth began to creak under the strain of imperfection. Adam cried out in discovered pain, "Oh wicked woman, what have I done to you that you have deprived me of the glory of God?" Adam blamed his wife, but deep down inside he knew it was his fault that he was no longer in perfect standing with the Lord Jah-el. Adam, upon realizing his nakedness, understood the reasoning behind his wife's covering of leaves and hastily followed suit. He came to understand the meaning of both good and evil. True they had become as Jah-el in this regard, but what they did not immediately understand was that from that moment they had begun to die. Adam and Eve ran to the remotest part of the Garden in an attempt to hide themselves. They had never experienced this gnawing sensation that was guilt. They were ashamed, and they hid. It was in this sad state of decline that Adam came to know his wife, to propagate his new-found imperfection to his offspring. In a now-imperfect world, in an unholy imperfect state, Eve became impregnated with the continuance of mankind in sin.

The third heaven was in an uproar. The angelic servants of Jah-el bemoaned that which had occurred before their eyes. They had watched the entire scenario from the kingdom of the third heaven. Jah-el had not interfered. Lucifer had chosen of his own volition to sin against Jah-el, but now he had tricked the human pair with his supernatural power and intellect. Had the human pair withstood the test, and rebuked the fallen cherub, Jah-el would have had ample reason to punish Lucifer on the spot. But he had not failed. Lucifer had now successfully persuaded the first human pair against Jahel's seat of authority. Lucifer had become a lying, deceiving, murderer. Because of his deceptive tactics, Lucifer had caused the death of the first human pair. By Adams own forfeiture was Lucifer now lord and ruler of the earth. The angels of heaven were appalled, and screamed for Lucifer's instant annihilation. Michael stood before his Creator awaiting the command of war, but there came no such decree. Lucifer had won this battle, but all intelligent creation was clueless that Lucifer's scheme had activated the plan of Jah-el set from before the founding of the world. This plan included the coming of a great and final future war between the sons of light and the sons of darkness, a war that Lucifer could never win, to recompense him fully for his villainy.

Jah-el thundered an assembly call of His heavenly host. They took their positions around His throne and He spoke, "You have witnessed the fall of man, and the fall of creation. You have seen the deception of the woman, by he who is the father of chaos. Lucifer has raised his hand against what is not his own, therefore he has raised his hand against Me. He has challenged My crowning creation—man, and it is through them that I shall bring Lucifer to his knees. Adam has lost Paradise, but I shall give his offspring the opportunity to regain it. Within the womb of Eve is already living the fruit of man. From mankind shall I also replenish to this My dominion, those that are fallen with Lucifer. I have not created the earth simply for nothing. Lucifer is already defeated, and has been since before the setting of the foundation of the world. This is but the beginning of the war between the called and the sons of darkness." Jah-el summoned Michael and said, "This is My decree. Proclaim to all of the angels of heaven that we are going to earth that I might pronounce judgment."

Michael did as Jah-el commanded. The four cherubim of the wheels lifted the throne chariot of Jah-el from the sea of crystal. They slowly guided the craft from the main hall, through the great expanse of the main doors of the vestibule, and into the outer reaches of the third heaven, a trail of billions upon billions of shining sparkling angels at the rear. The throne chariot moved toward and through the alpha portal. Jah-el entered into the finite world of the second heaven, He and his multitude of angels. Once outside Jah-el gave His command, and with the movement of lightning the four cherubim of the wheels streaked the throne chariot to its destination.

The throne chariot of Jah-el stopped just short of entering earth's atmosphere, the first heaven. Jah-el's chariot hovered above the vast sea of water that was suspended around the earth. At His command a multitude of the angelic beings of God passed through into the first heaven, blasting trumpets, singing hymns, and praises, announcing the coming of the Creator of the universe. The Lord Jah-el caused His chariot to set down in His Garden, over the tree of life, and when He did every form of vegetation on the earth burst forth into flower. Jah-el called out to Adam saying, "Adam, where are you? Can the house be hidden from the very presence of its builder?" Adam sheepishly answered, "I hear Your voice my Father, and it is not that I do not wish to come before You, but I am afraid because I am naked." Jah-el spoke again to His crowning creation saying, "Who has told you that you are naked? Have you eaten of the tree of which I commanded you not to eat?" Adam attempted to shift the weight of his guilt to his wife, and to Jah-el Himself saying, "The woman that You gave me Lord Jah-el, she gave me of the fruit and of it I ate." Eve was not to be outdone, and she passed the guilt to the serpent saying, "Lord Jah-el the serpent deceived me, and I ate of the tree."

Jah-el turned His attention to the very serpent chosen of Lucifer, and pronounced upon it a judgment that would also impact every serpent throughout creation. Jah-el decreed, "Because you were the instrument of Lucifer you are cursed above all cattle, and above every beast of the field. Upon your belly you will crawl, and dust shall you eat all the days of your life." Jah-el stripped it of its legs, wings, ears, and power of speech. Jah-el split the serpent's tongue. There was no mercy in this decree of the Lord of hosts.

At this point everything on earth was silent. Nothing dared to make a sound as the God of the universe pronounced judgment. Adam and his wife stood before their Lord, heads dropped low, tears streaming down their cheeks. As Jah-el continued to rumble forth His divine displeasure, Eve sobbed uncontrollably. She sought the closeness of her husband for security, as they wondered of their outcome in complete terror. Before their eyes the physical form of the serpent had been radically altered; it was horrid. What was once a proud and special creation of Jah-el was now nothing more than an oversized worm, writhing and twisting on the ground before them. Jah-el paused for a moment, Adam and Eve cringing and locked in fear at this sliver of silence. Without warning the Creator of all things raised His mighty hand and brought it crashing down on the arm of His sapphire-blue throne, bellowing forth in summons the name Lucifer. Adam and his wife fell to the ground, trembling uncontrollably, bewildered, their faces smashed into the earth, their arms and elbows locked about their heads.

There was silence, eerie silence. Adam peeked upwards from beneath the protective shielding of his hands. He gathered enough nerve to raise himself to a kneeling position. There above him, and all around him were the angels of Jah-el. On either side of Him were stationed two cherubs. The angels of Jah-el stood or hovered in their places, their faces fixed upon what was now an invisible throne of Jah-el. It was obvious to Adam that they could see what he could not. He could hear the voice of God, but he could no longer see His blinding presence. What was to occur next was not for the eyes of the first human pair. It was meant only for the invisible realm. Jah-el had summoned someone that Adam and Eve did not directly know—Lucifer and all his following, to pronounce judgment.

The Lord Jah-el lifted His head at the sight coming toward Him. "Still the same Lucifer," He thought as He remembered a similar meeting in the third heaven. How proud and defiant this cherub named Lucifer. Lucifer kept his distance, for Michael, Gabriel, Raphael, and Uriel were stationed at the extremities of the throne platform. Lucifer and his host hovered before Jah-el. Jah-el peered forth at His fallen cherub and said in a voice exuding doom, "Come a little ways forward thou wicked serpent." In the invisible realm Lucifer proceeded closer to the throne. In the visible realm Adam watched as the serpent snaked closer to the location of the now invisible throne chariot. Adam was amazed, as he pulled his wife to her knees he whispered, "Eve witness this event, for the Lord Jah-el is not finished with the judgment of the serpent." Jah-el raised His mighty voice to the pitch of thunderclaps, His finger pointing toward Lucifer in a gesture of condemnation. "I shall put enmity between you and the woman, and between your seed and her seed. He shall bruise you in thy head, and you shall bruise Him in His heel." In the invisible Lucifer and his host, and all the angelic beings of Jah-el were puzzled as to this statement by Jah-el. In the visible, Adam and his wife shared the same bewilderment, "What woman? What seed? What enmity? What bruising?" Lucifer hovered before the Lord of hosts, agonizing over the meaning of this mystery spoken by God, and then it began to happen. The throne of Jah-el took on a fiery pulsating glow as had not been seen by the angels since Jah-el created the portals of the third heaven and the finite world. The shield wings of the twenty-four and sixteen winged cherubim instinctively shot into position, as well as those of the seraphim. The ophanim backed further away from the presence of the Most High. The fallen angels cowered in increased fear, but Lucifer stood his ground. Lucifer had a front row seat to the answer of a mystery he had wondered about when he was yet in his position of glory in the third heaven. The mystery of the three pitches of thunder was about to be revealed.

The cherubim and seraphim peeked from behind their shield wings. The ophanim looked on from their place of safety. The fallen angels and their leader Lucifer stared in statue-like awe at the spectacle transpiring before their eyes. Jah-el was splitting apart, di-viding, no tri-viding! Jah-el was in actuality three! All present in that spiritual realm witnessed the mystery of mysteries. They began to under-stand what Jah-el meant when He had said, "Let Us make man in Our own image." Jah-el was three in one, and one in three. The angels of the Most High burst forth in song and praise. They blasted their trumpets and praised the mystery that was Jah-el. In the visible realm Adam and Eve, once again upon their feet, stood motionless, wondering at such a commotion. Invisible before that assembly stood God the Father Jah-el, His face glowing the white-hot color of heated iron, His face ineffable, marvelous and terrible to look upon, emitting sparks and rays that far surpass even the brightest star. To Jah-el's right stood another being, one who was in appearance like a son of man whose face was full of graciousness. This one was in appearance as adorned in the purest of white, and His countenance shone as the bright-ness of the sun. To Jah-el's left stood yet another being whose definition was formless, but who radiated untold power and might, a spirit being—an intelligent entity of personality and character, a formless force. Lucifer recoiled in trepidation, his followers disbanded in alarm as the three separate entities reunited into their oneness, and the voice of Jah-el commanded, "Serpent, be gone! No longer shall your name be called Lucifer, but Satan, the devil, for you are a liar, the father of the lie, a murderer, and a manslayer. Satan, be gone!" In the visible Adam and his wife watched as the serpent slithered away, puzzled with the names by which Jah-el had addressed it.

At that moment the Lord Jah-el reappeared before Adam and his wife. The instantaneous transfusion of His brightness to the eyes of the first human pair sent them crashing to the dust on their knees, their faces encased once again in the protection of their hands. Jah-el was not compassionate for His edict had been disobeyed. He fired forth His judgment upon Eve and decreed, "Eve, because you have transgressed the mandate set forth from My mouth, I will greatly multiply your sorrow in your conception, and in sorrow and pain shall you bring forth your children. Your longing shall always be after your husband, and he shall rule over you." Then Jah-el turned His attention to His marvel of marvels, the man Adam, His image, and said, "Adam, because you did listen to the voice of your wife and have eaten of the tree of which I commanded you not to eat, cursed is the ground because of you. In sorrow shall you eat of it all the days of your life. Thorns and thistles shall the earth bring forth for you, and you shall eat the herbs of the field. By the sweat of your labor shall you eat bread till you return to the ground from whence I made you, for out of dust were you taken, and to dust you shall return!"

After the pronouncement of judgment upon the first

human pair, the Lord Jah-el made coats of skin to cover their nakedness. The Lord Jah-el spoke within Himself saying, "Behold the man has become as one of Us, knowing good and evil. Let Us cast him forth out of the Garden lest he put his hand forward and partake of the tree of life and live forever." Then Jah-el spoke and commanded a contingent of angels to cast Adam and his wife from the Garden of Eden. As they were being driven from the Garden, Adam and his wife wailed aloud in dire lamentation. Adam begged the angels not to cast him from his home without allowing him to first make entreaty to Jah-el for mercy. The angels, moved with pity, ceased to drive Adam out. Adam came forth and threw himself before Jah-el, begging and pleading for the pardoning of his sin. Then Jah-el directed His attention to his angels and said, "Why have you ceased from driving this wicked man from Paradise? Why are you not casting him out? Is it I who have done wrong? Or is My judgment judged badly?" Then the angels of Jah-el bowed themselves low on the ground of Paradise and worshipped Jah-el saying, "You are just O Lord, and your judgment is righteous." Jah-el turned His gaze to Adam sniveling before Him and decreed, "I will not suffer you from this moment forward to be in Paradise." Adam returned saying, "Please grant me O Lord of the tree of life that I may eat of it, before You have me cast out." Then Jah-el answered His corporeal son explaining, "Adam you shall not eat of the tree of life now, for I have commanded the cherubim with the flaming sword that turns every which way to guard it from you that you may not partake. My son, you are now involved in a war in which your adversary has caused you to be. If when you are gone out from this Paradise you should keep yourself from further evil as one about to die, when the resurrection shall come to be I will raise you up from death and allow you to partake of the tree." Jah-el once again ordered the ousting of Adam and his wife, but Adam continued his weeping and protest. The angel closest to Adam sympathet-ically burst forth in a question of impotence asking, "What would you have us do Adam? The Lord Jah-el has decreed!" Adam, through his anguished tears, pleaded saying, "I know that you must cast me from my home, but I pray you to allow me to take fragrant herbs from this place that I may make an offering to Jah-el after my expulsion."

The angel looked toward the seat of God with pity in his eyes, because the angels of Jah-el loved the human pair. The angel cried out in a loud voice beseeching saying, "Jah-el, Eternal King, please command me your servant that there be given to Adam your son, sweet incense of odor from Paradise." And Jah-el bade Adam to take with him from Paradise four kinds of fragrant herbs they being crocus, nard, cinnamon, and calamus. After taking these were they cast from the Garden.

Adam and Eve stood outside of what was once their beautiful home. There was nothing on the outside to compare with that on the inside. The vegetation was in tumbled disarray. There were no well-kept paths, and outside of the Garden lived animals of gigantic proportion. Because of their sin, creation had fallen. At the moment Adam ate of the fruit, all of the produce had fallen to the earth rotted. The animal life of earth had begun to act strangely. There was now discord in the earth. It was now the domain of Lucifer, and the perfect balance of Jah-el ceased to operate at full capacity. Throughout the jungle could be heard cries of pain, as the larger animal life took advantage of the smaller. Because of the shortage of food and the imbalance of imperfection, many of the beasts of the earth would deviate from their normal diet. Carrion eaters and some herbivores alike would become live flesh eaters. With no berries or seed pocketed fruit to sustain them, the fowl of the air began to prey on insects. The character of sea life was changed that it began to devour one another. It would not wax better as time progressed, but worse. Jah-el knew that Adam and his wife would and could survive outside the Garden. He knew that they would multiply, fill, and replenish the earth. He knew that some would serve Him as their Master, while others would follow the path of mutinous Lucifer. He knew everything and from those He knew would serve Him would be chosen the called, those whom He would use throughout this crack in infinity to perpetuate His plan—the plan that would eternally right the wrong. Adam and his wife stood there as if rooted in that spot, just outside of the entrance of Paradise. There was no way for them to return for stationed at the entrance were two cherubim, and a flaming sword spun around the Garden at indescribable speed causing a field of energy that would mean certain death to anyone attempting to penetrate. As they stood there in this foreign world they heard the angels of Jah-el blast their trumpets, and with the swiftness that is unperceivable to the human eye Jah-el departed His planet Earth. Save for the staid mute cherubim at the gate of Paradise, Adam and Eve were now completely alone.

CHAPTER 4

THE BIRTH OF TIME

A dam had dwelt in the Paradise planted by Jah-el, the place called Eden, for sixty-nine years. In the sixty-ninth year of Adam's life he did sin. In the sixty-ninth year of Adam's life was offspring conceived by his wife Eve. In the sixty-ninth year of Adam's life was judgment pronounced upon he and his wife, and they were cast from the Garden. For sixty-nine years had the marvel of marvels remained in the perfect will of Jah-el. Now he was an outcast.

Adam and Eve both realized that return to their garden home was hopeless. Being finally reconciled to this fact, they made for themselves a shelter close by the entrance and they mourned and lamented for seven days. After seven days they felt the first twinges of hunger, and began to search their immediate surroundings for food but found none. Eve said to Adam, "My husband, I am hungry. Go and search further for something of which we may eat." Adam arose and searched for an additional seven days, but found no food such as they were accustomed to in the Garden. Adam returned empty-handed to his wife, and in her despair

Eve pleaded to her husband saying, "Adam, take my life please. Kill me that I may die and perhaps the Lord Jah-el will admit you once again to Eden, for it is on my account that you have been cast out." Adam shuddered at such a thought, and soothingly answered his wife saying, "My beloved wife, please refrain from such foolish words for fear that Jah-el may bring upon us a further curse. How is it possible that I should take the life of my own flesh? I would never do such a thing. No, let us continue searching for something to live on that we fail not."

Adam and his wife searched an additional nine days but still found nothing as they were accustomed to in Paradise, but found only the food eaten by the beasts of the earth. They had been without sustenance for twenty-three days. Adam said to his wife, "Eve, it is only just and right that we should lament before the sight of God who made us. Let us repent with a great penitence, and perhaps Jah-el will take pity on us and cause His angels to bring us food." Eve questioned Adam with a look of dismay, "What is penitence? Tell me, what sort of penitence am I to do?" Adam said to his wife, "We must show Jah-el that we are remorseful of our sin, and that we are in need of His divine aid. Eve, you cannot do as much as I for I shall stand forty days in the river Gi'hon. How many days will you stand? Do only as much as you have strength." Eve replied, "I shall stand for thirty-seven days."

The offerings of the fragrant spices to the Lord Jah-el as an open display of their remorse had not gained them anything; heaven remained silent. "Perhaps this sacrifice will move Jah-el to compassion," Adam said to his wife. He continued saying, "Eve, go to the river Tigris and place a stone in the river, one that will allow you to stand in its waters up to the neck. Let no speech proceed from your mouth, for we are unworthy to address the Lord of hosts, and do stand in the river's water for thirty-seven days. Go now, that the Lord Jah-el may have mercy on us."

Eve walked to the river Tigris and did as Adam had instructed. Likewise, Adam walked to the river Gi'hon and stood on a stone up to his neck in the water. Adam then said these words only at the beginning of his penitence, "I tell you waters of Gi'hon grieve with me, and assemble to me all swimming creatures which are in you and let them surround me and mourn in company with me. Not for themselves should they be in sorrow, but for me. For it is I who have sinned, and fallen short of the glory of Jah-el." The creatures of the river obeyed the voice of Adam and surrounded him, and forthwith the current of the river was stayed and stood still.

Lucifer sat in marked silence, his angels around him. In his domain of gloom, the dark lord reflected on the events of the recent past. He was puzzled and amazed. Jah-el was three, and somehow the One that stood to the right of Jah-el would cause him harm. How? The fallen angels under Lucifer's command had been assured of their doom. Jah-el's words, once spoken were final. Jah-el had prophesied their fate. Lucifer knew his time was short but in the time he had he vowed to take as many of mankind as he could with him. Lucifer commanded an audience that all of his angels come in to him and he said, "This is my decree. Jah-el has prophesied our coming demise. He has ordained that in a future time, I am to be bruised in the head by He that has the appearance of the son of man. We shall not remain idle in the earth but shall wreak havoc upon it, and devastate it. We shall mislead men as I misled Eve, and that weak creature Adam. If we are to suffer punishment, then men shall also. From this time forward man is our enemy, therefore let us swear an oath to his annihilation." All of the fallen angels swore such an oath. The descendants of Adam would soon taste of the manifold malignancy that is Satan.

In the cold and gloomy place that is the kingdom of the dark lord, Lucifer sat. He was in deep meditations of evil when one of his generals, the angel Semjazael, brought him the report of Adam and Eve's exercise of repentance. Lucifer exploded in turbulent rage, "I shall put an end to this," and forthwith departed his kingdom.

Eighteen days of their penitence had drifted painfully into the past of both the lives of the first human pair. Lucifer arrived at the place of Eve's exercise of penitence, and immediately transformed himself from his true vestige of vileness to that of the brightness of an holy angel. Lucifer glided to the river's edge and found Eve weeping, her tears melting into the waters just below her chin. Lucifer pretending to share in Eve's grief also began to weep and said to her, "Come out of the river and lament no more. Cease from your sorrow. There is no longer any reason to be anxious. The Lord has heard the plea of you and your husband and has accepted your penitence. We the angels of heaven entreated on your behalf, and have made supplication before His throne concerning you. Be of good cheer, for He has sent me to bring you out of the river's water and give you the nourishment that you so desire. Now come up out of the water and I shall take you to the feast that He has made ready."

Eve heard and believed and came out of the river Tigris, her flesh trembling like wind-blown grass. She fell to the earth faint, but Lucifer reached out to her and lifted her to her feet. He escorted her to the bank of the river Gi'hon. Eve, upon seeing her husband, cried out to him in a voice of relief saying, "Adam my husband, the Lord Jah-el has heard our plea." Adam lifted his head toward the voice of his wife, and upon seeing her with the cherub he broke forth in a mournful wail crying, "Oh Eve, Eve, where is the labor of your penitence? How is it that you have been ensnared once more by our adversary?" When Eve heard this she understood that the angel standing next to her was the same angel that had deceived her prior. Eve fell to the earth on her knees, redoubled in anguish, crying out, "Woe to you cherub, whoever you are! Why do you attack us for no reason? What have we done to you that you keep pursuing us with craft? For what do we deserve such maliciousness?" Adam, from his station in the river, called forth to the cherub standing beside his wife. Lucifer turned his gaze to the pitiable sight neck deep in the river. In the most-weary of voices Adam asked, "Angel of the order cherubim, why do you persecute us?"

Lucifer released a heavy sigh and answered saying, "Adam you are the cause of all my hostility, envy, and sorrow, since it is because of you that I have been expelled from heaven, and all of the angels at my command." Adam recoiled in shock. Eve stood with her mouth agape, attempting to digest the information coming from the angel. Adam continued, stammering, "What have I done to you? What fault is it that you hold to my account, seeing that you have received no harm or injury from us? Why do you torment us?"

Lucifer replied, "Adam, are you telling me that you do not know? Adam, it is because of you that I am here. The Lord Jah-el commanded me here, awaiting your creation. Upon your creation He sent to me, and the company of angels with me, Michael the archangel. Michael came to us with the commandment of Jah-el that we were to be the watchers of paradise, and your servants. I was required to bow before you Adam, in semblance of servitude to you, but

I refused. Michael continued to say to me the decree of Jah-el for you are His image creation, but I would not bow before you a younger being than myself. When the angels that were at my command heard me, they too refused the decree. Michael was astonished at my refusal, and said to me, Lucifer, bow before the image of Jah-el or else He will be displeased with you. I said, I care not if Jah-el be displeased, for if He be wroth with me then I will set my seat above the stars of heaven, and I will be just like Jah-el."

The past events suddenly and nauseatingly began making partial sense to Adam and his wife. Eve understood the reason for her deception. Adam understood that at the judgment of the serpent, Jah-el was in actuality speaking to this fallen cherub standing before him. He understood that this one with whom he conversed was Satan, the devil, the manslayer and father of the lie, he that was called Lucifer before Jah-el's decree of the changing of his name. But the matter of enmity and bruising still plagued his mind. It was obvious that Jah-el had a scheme of things planned for the future, but what? It took only a split second for both Adam and his wife to come to these realizations. They grasped and digested between the sentences that Lucifer expounded. Lucifer continued saying, "Jah-el summoned us to heaven by His own voice and passed judgment upon us for the first sin. Jah-el was angered by our insubordination and for it we were cast into this world. Straightaway we were overcome with grief because we had lost our great glory. We became increasingly incensed at your divine joy and luxury. So with guile I deceived your wife and caused your expulsion, that you may be as we."

When Adam heard the angel say these words he screamed at the top of his lungs, straining his vocal cords in a dirge of despair, "Oh Lord my God, my life is in Your hands. Please Jah-el banish this adversary far from me, he who seeks to destroy my soul. Please Jah-el, grant me his glory that he himself has lost." At that moment Satan vanished from before the first human pair, satisfied that he had caused sufficient grief. Adam was enlightened, and that illumination had caused him to know the awful truth. He had been tricked. He had been made a pawn of the evil one. Something stirred deep inside of him, something that would stir down through the corridor of time inside of each individual who would become one of the called. The thing that was stirring was an emotion. The emotion was hatred, hatred of Satan and his evil. It was true that Satan hated man, but now it was also true that there was a man who hated Satan. Adam had learned the awful truth. He was no longer ignorant, but informed. Adam stood numb in the waters of the river Gi'hon. He had found renewed strength in his hatred and with teeth clenched, Adam endured his penitence, standing for forty days in the river.

At the end of the forty-day period Adam emerged from the waters. He stumbled onto the bank and lay as if dead. Eve came to him and placed his head upon her lap. Malnourishment was taking its toll. Adam and his wife had not eaten for some sixty-three days, and their bodies bore the evidence of their abstinence. Adam and Eve were exhausted. He from the labor of his penitence, she from agonizing their loss of Paradise and the favor of Jah-el. Eve crumbled backwards from her sitting position, her long hair soaked in mud. She could not go on any longer. Adam opened his swollen eyes first in a squint, then gradually to full sight. His wife's legs and thighs were cut and bruised by the many thorns and thistles that had seemed to spring up from nowhere. He reached, searching the silt, and found Eve's small and fragile hand. He caressed it gently and whispered to her, "It is better that we die Eve. For the earth is inhospitable towards us." At that moment a bright light appeared before them, and they heard a familiar voice. It was Michael the merciful, the archangel. Michael glided toward the first human pair, his eyes full of compassion. Hot tears of pain and joy welled up and ran down the cheeks of Adam and his wife, Michael's presence serving as assurance that Jah-el had answered their plea of penitence.

In His divine mercy Jah-el decreed a miraculous, though temporary, provision of sustenance to Adam and his wife, until such a time as the earth would again support them. It would not be much longer, for at the time of Jah-el's arrival on the earth every type of vegetation had burst into bloom, and ripened fruit was soon forthcoming. Jah-el's miraculous provision brought great comfort to Adam and his wife, for they both concluded that while they were now unholy in the sight of God was He yet still mindful of them. He had not totally abandoned them. Adam and his wife soon regained their vigor, and set about finding a place of permanent shelter.

Adam and his wife settled in the land of Elda, which means land of nativity, in the vicinity of the Garden, in a cave in the side of one of the camel-humped hills they had once viewed from Paradise. In the third month of their ousting, in the seventieth year of Adam's life, Eve said to her husband, "Adam I pray to the Lord Jah-el that you should live, that you should be restored to Paradise since you did not commit either the first or the second error. I can no longer abide and watch your hard labor. It is unfair, for it is I who have erred. Adam my husband, please banish me from your presence. Order me to depart that I may go away and await death." The love that Adam felt surged inside and he embraced Eve, and soothed her once more saying, "Dear Eve, you who are bone of my bone and flesh of my flesh, I bear this curse because I have sinned before Jah-el. You and

I have sinned mutually." At the close of that day the first human pair retired to their place of resting but Eve could not sleep. Guilt gnawed at her every waking moment. She could not tolerate it any longer and while her husband slept, she departed from him.

Eve began to walk towards the west, weeping bitterly and mourning aloud. She took every precaution to cover her trail, for she was convinced that her absence from Adam would secure his reinstatement to Paradise. Toward the noon of the third day's walk, Eve chose a spot and there proceeded to build for herself a shelter. She had brought with her sufficient of the miraculous provision to hopefully sustain her till the ripening of the vegetation of the earth, for its time was close at hand. At the evening of that third day Eve reclined for the night's sleep, her hands resting on her fattening belly. In her womb was offspring of three months old.

Adam was frantic upon his next day's awakening to the departure of his beloved Eve. In his wife's emotional state he was unsure what she would do, or had done. He searched the land for clues as to his wife's whereabouts, but found none. Stark cold reality impacted his dazed mind like the thundering of Jah-el's voice; Eve was gone and he could not find her. He cried aloud towards heaven seeking a message from the Lord of spirits, but not one of the holy angels appeared to him. Adam was in solitary once again, and it was not to his liking.

Eve struggled through the following three months. She allotted her provisions most sparingly. At times she ate vegetation not becoming to a human being, but it sustained her. It gave her stomach something on which to function. She became increasingly elated as the fruit trees approached their season of edibility. Some of the fruit she had eaten before its time had pained her, but she was surviving. She thought of her husband often, wondering what he might be doing and if the Lord Jah-el had restored him to His perfect favor due to her absence. Eve was now six months with child, her abdomen distended. She toyed with its increasing roundness. She knew that what was inside was alive and like herself. She had watched the animals of the earth give birth, and the offspring was always like its parents. She was ecstatic in her anticipation. Then something engulfed her. A longing. She wanted her husband. She was becoming afraid. What would she do when it came time to give birth? Who would be with her?

When the time of her bearing approached she began to be distressed with great pain, and she cried aloud between intervals, "Pity me O Lord, assist me please." But Jah-el would not hear her, and the mercy of God did not encircle her. Eve began to moan to herself, saying, "Who shall tell my husband Adam? I implore you angels of heaven, at what time you should return to the east, please bear a message to my husband." In that same hour a vision of the complaint of his wife came to him, and the place of her residence. Adam said to himself, "Perhaps once more the serpent is tormenting her." Adam, as soon as he saw, went forth into the wilderness, two day's journey, and found his wife in excruciating pain. As he approached, Eve cried out in joy, her arms opened wide. Adam was visibly shaken by the sight which greeted him. Was this the same Eve, her belly protruded and bloated? Adam, by process of association, realized that he was soon to be a parent. Human procreation was nigh to fruition. Adam kneeled at his wife's side, kissing and scolding her in unison. He was so happy to see her, and she him. Eve blurted forth uncontrollably, "My husband, from the moment I saw you coming towards me my grief-laden soul was refreshed. Please Adam speak to the Lord on my behalf, He will listen to your voice. Ask Him my husband to have mercy on me, and free me from these awful pains."

Adam knelt, crying aloud the plight of his wife before Jah-el. And behold there came twelve angels from heaven, six on the right side and six on the left side of Eve. Michael was among the six stationed on the right, and glided over to Eve and began to stroke her comfortingly about her face. As he did, Michael said to Eve, "Blessed are you Eve, for Adam's sake. Since his prayers and intercession for you are great, I have been sent that you might receive help. Rise up now and prepare to bear." And Eve bore a son, and he was beautiful. Eve adored her newborn son and she called his name Cain. And Eve continued in her joy saying, "It is with the help of the Lord that I have birthed a man."

After the birth of Cain, his son, Adam took his wife and child back to the land of their dwelling in the east. Adam began to work the ground and to plant in abundance the seeds of such varieties as they were used to in Paradise.

Shortly thereafter, in the seventy-eighth year of Adam's life, Eve conceived and bore another son and they called his name Abel. Cain the older, and Abel the younger grew in size and stature. When Cain was sixteen years of age, and his brother Abel eight, Eve received a vision in a dream. Upon awakening, she was greatly troubled by this dream and at once recounted it to Adam saying, "My husband, last night while we were yet sleeping, a distressing and terrible dream came to me. I saw in this dream the blood of our son Abel being poured into the mouth of our son Cain, and he was drinking it without remorse. But Abel begged him to leave him a little of it that he might not perish, but Cain hearkened not to his plea but drank it all to the last drop.

And what is even more awful is that the blood of our son Abel Cain could not hold in his bowels, and it came gushing forth from his mouth." And Adam sat puzzled before his wife as to the meaning of the dream, then he said, "Alas if Cain should kill his brother Abel, for what reason? Yet let us separate them from one another, and let us make for them separate places of dwelling." Thus Adam made Cain a husbandman, a tiller of the soil, and his son Abel he made a shepherd that they might be mutually separated.

In the process of time, it came to pass that Cain brought of the fruit of the ground as an offering to the Lord. Abel his brother proceeded to do likewise, and made an offering before the Lord Jah-el of a firstling of his flock and the fat thereof. And the Lord had respect toward Abel's sacrifice because of the shedding of the blood. But to Cain and his sacrifice Jah-el gave no respect, and Cain was filled with anger. Jah-el spoke to Cain in a voice from heaven and said, "Cain why are you angry and why is your disposition changed to that of hate? If you sacrifice to Me as your brother has, will I not be as pleased with you also?" Cain would not be consoled; after all, he was the elder. How dare Jah-el accept his younger brother's offering and not his? Cain was now under the influence of the evil one, the one called Satan. Satan proceeded to whisper into the ear of Cain malicious thoughts concerning Jah-el. Satan taunted, "Who is this voice from heaven that He may choose to over-look you? Why should you have to present a second sacrifice like that of your younger brother?" Cain was at his wit's end. He stood before Jah-el, his fist and teeth clenched vise-like. His insides boiled. His sanity erased for a fleeting moment, Satan introduced into his mind the thought of a most heinous crime. Satan suggested, "If Jah-el so loves Abel, and not you, then take the life of who is dear. It is above you to take example from he that is inferior in years."

As Satan continued his torment of the mind of Cain a wicked regression of thought was formulated. Cain emotionally, then mentally, began transferring the cause of his sacrifice's rejection first from himself, then onto Jah-el, and then finally onto his brother Abel. Satan had successfully warped Cain's mind. Cain said, "It is because of Abel that I am not in favor with the Lord," and so heeding the voice of evil Cain vowed, "I shall kill my brother."

The voice of Jah-el continued speaking a warning to Cain. Jah-el knew the destructive course of Cain's thoughts and He warned, "Cain, if you do not turn from the wickedness stored in your heart then sin is waiting to pounce upon you and to devour you. Listen not to the evil one spoken of to you by Adam your father for he is a liar, the father of lies, and an ensnarer of the souls of men."

After conversing with the Lord of heaven, Cain left his place of sacrifice to search for his brother Abel. Cain would not heed the righteous admonition of the Lord Jah-el. It was fixed in his heart what he would do. He was convinced that he hated Abel and because of it, Abel must die.

Cain stood a little ways off from his younger brother, hiding amongst the tall corn he had planted. He watched as Abel conversed with the Lord in prayer. He perceived the flat rock where lay the slaughtered lamb of Abel's sacrifice, its life's blood spilt. He saw how Abel had disemboweled the lamb, and laid its inward parts before the facc of the Lord. He saw the sharp rock that was the instrument of slaughter, it being crimson with the shed blood of the lamb. Cain called out to his brother, interrupting his prayer. Abel got up off his knees to greet his brother, a smile of innocence gracing his lips. He opened his arms to embrace his brother, but Cain returned no such endearment. Cain, then bending his arms upwards from the elbow, grasped the arms of his brother, forcefully breaking off Abel's embrace. Cain proceeded to tell Abel of his experience and part of his communication with the Lord Jah-el; how Jah-el had found favor with Abel's sacrifice and not with his own. Abel showered genuine brotherly concern toward the obvious pain that such a rejection had caused. He would aid his brother in any way possible, to help him attain a correct standing with the Lord of hosts. Abel entreated his brother in all honesty, asking, "Brother, how might I aid you in returning to the peace of your former self prior to the lesson of the sacrifice?" Feigning true interest Cain implored, "Abel, my brother, will you make known to me the way of preparing the offering of the lamb."

Abel, being more than eager to share with his brother, turned his back to him and squatted before his makeshift altar. As he was making explanation to his brother, he did not see Cain pick up the sharp rock of slaughter. Cain raised the rock high above his head, and brought it crashing down on the unsuspecting skull of his brother. The sound was horrifying, as bone gave way to the impact of stone. Abel emitted a blood-curdling scream in acknowledgment of the blow. He fell backwards from the perch of his squatted position, and as he did his stunned eyes met those of his enraged older brother. In them he witnessed something he had never seen before—Cain's eyes were glazed, his face contorted, his breathing rapid. He was ranting to the top of his lungs his hatred. Abel lay dazed upon the ground, his limbs uncoordinated, and as he attempted to bring his hands to the wound in his head, Cain savagely rammed the stone into his brother's left temple. Abel began pleading with his brother, all the while attempting to understand the unexplainable, tears of suffering and confusion streaming from his eyes, mingling with his blood, dropping and being absorbed into the ground. "Cain, please don't hurt me anymore," Abel managed to entreat, but there was no mercy to be found in Cain. Cain stood astraddle his brother, screaming, "Don't hurt you! Don't hurt you! I have not yet begun to hurt you Abel. Cry out to Jah-el, since you are His favorite. Pray Him to save you from my hand!" Abel lifted his eyes toward heaven but before he could utter another sound, Cain beat him brutally about the head and face. Abel died at the hands of Cain, and in Cain's heart was no remorse. Cain attempted to cover his brother's body with rocks, but with each attempt the rocks would roll away. Finally, out of sheer desperation, Cain took his brother's body to a thicket of brambles and cast him therein.

Cain was in his fields tending them, when the voice of Jah-el once again spoke to him saying, "Cain, where is thy brother Abel?" Cain answered in a voice of indignation, "How should I know? Am I my brother's keeper?" Jah-el continued to speak saying, "What have you done Cain, that your brother's blood cries out to Me from the ground? Now you are cursed from the earth, which has opened her mouth to receive Abel's blood. When you till the earth Cain, from henceforth she will not produce for you. A fugitive and a roamer you shall be in the earth." Cain recoiled at the severity of His judgment and complained to Jah-el, "My punishment is more than I can bear. You are actually driving me this day from off the surface of the earth, and from Your face I am concealed. It is certain that anyone finding me shall kill me because of my crime." Jah-el spoke once more to the murderer cringing before him and said, "Any man slaying you Cain, I shall require a seven-fold vengeance on him." Then the Lord Jah-el struck Cain in the center of his forehead and caused a mark upon him, so that any man finding Cain would not slay him; thus was the decree of Jah-el. Cain went tumbling backwards in the dust, his hand placed

upon the mark of Jah-el in his forehead. He scrambled, flee-
ing from before Jah-el's face. He fled into the wilderness
away from his mother and father. He was a marked man,
and the guilt of his crime was evident by the mark he wore.

Toward the twilight of the day, Adam went searching for
his sons. After searching the caves of both Cain and Abel he
returned to his wife, troubled by their disappearance. Eve
knew by her maternal instinct that something was amiss.
She kept her worse fears to herself. The dream that she had
those many years before was now back to haunt her. "Abel
is dead," she thought, "Cain has killed Abel." Eve was
awakened from her trancelike state by the voice of her
husband Adam. Adam was speaking to her in an attempt to
allay her fears. He knew all too well what his wife was
thinking, the misting of her eyes being conclusive evidence.
Adam said, "Let us retire and gain our rest, that on the
morrow we may arise and see what has become of our sons.
Perhaps our adversary is assailing them somewhere."

Adam and his wife arose early. They went first to the
camp of their youngest son, crying out his name, "Abel,
Abel, where are you?" There was no answer. They walked
further into the grazing meadow of the sheep. There they
came to the altar site, the sacrificial lamb still lying there.
Adam stood, surveying the sight before him. There was too
much blood in the area to come only from the small lamb
slaughtered there before him. The site was in obvious disarray. There were signs of violence everywhere. Their worst
fear was a reality, and they both knew it. The vision had
come true. Cain had killed his brother. Eve collapsed into
the arms of her husband, succumbing to the horror of what
she knew to be the truth. They searched just a little ways
further, and found their son's body immersed in the bramble
thicket. They sat at the perimeter of this rambling mass of

thorn-laden vegetation weeping, wailing, and throwing handfuls of dust into the air, anguished by the sight of their battered son before them.

Jah-el sat in the third heaven upon His throne of majesty; He and his faithful angels watched the pitiable sight of what was taking place on earth. Jah-el summoned Michael His angel of might, and said, "Michael, I have a mission of mercy for you. Go to the earth and say this to My son Adam. Tell him he is not to grieve the loss of Abel for I shall give to him another son in his stead, and that son will bring him great joy." Michael carried out the decree of Jah-el and relayed to Adam all that the Lord of Spirits decreed. Adam received the counsel and the promise of Jah-el with gladness, and he kept the words of God in his heart. But still they grieved, for Abel was no more to be numbered amongst them.

At the time of Cain's murdering Abel, Cain was thirty years of age and his brother twenty-two. Adam, their father, was then one hundred years old. Cain had settled in the land of Nod, a land located to the east of Elda and the Garden of Eden. Prior when Adam was eighty-five years of age Eve had also bore him a daughter, and they called her name Awan.

Adam once again knew his wife, and in the one hundred and thirtieth year of his existence Eve bore him the promised son. Adam said to his wife in ecstatic joy, "See! We have begotten a son in place of our slain son Abel. Let us give glory and sacrifice to the gracious Lord Jah-el." Adam called his son Seth.

When Adam was one hundred and forty-two years of age, Eve bore him another daughter and they called her name Azura. In the one hundred ninety-sixth year of Adam's existence Cain journeyed from his land of Nod, back to the land of his birth, and took for himself a wife, namely his sister Awan. Cain returned once again to his land of Nod for there was no place found for him in Elda, the land of his birth, and there he sired children and became a builder of cities.

And this is the continuation of the history of man. When Adam was two hundred and thirty-two years of age, Seth took his sister Azura as his wife. In the two hundred and thirty-fifth year of Adam's existence, Seth begat a son by Azura and they called his name Enos. Seth was one hundred and five years old at the birth of his son. When Adam was three hundred and twenty-one years of age, Enos took to wife his sister Noam. When Enos was ninety years of age, and Adam was three hundred and twenty-five, Cainan was born to Enos and Naom. When Adam was three hundred and ninety-two years of age, Cainan took to wife his sister Mualeleth. When Cainan was seventy years of age, and Adam three hundred and ninety-five, Mualeleth bore a son to Cainan, and they called his name Mahalalel. When Adam was four hundred and fifty-eight years of age Mahalalel took to wife Dinah, the daughter of Barakiel his father's brother. When Mahalalel was sixty-five years of age, and Adam four hundred and sixty, Dinah bore to Mahalalel a son, and they called his name Jared.

At the birth of Jared lived Adam and his wife Eve, Cain and his wife Awan, Seth and his wife Azura, Enos and his wife Naom, Cainan and his wife Mualeleth, Mahalalel and his wife Dinah, and the multitude of all the additional sons and daughters too numerous to name, birthed in the four hundred and sixty years of mankind's existence from the ousting from Paradise. Since the days of Enos men in the earth had begun to formally worship the Lord of Spirits, Jah-el, but now something unfathomably devastating was about to occur on earth. Men would soon come face to face with the Evil Watchers.

CHAPTER 5

I ENOCH

In the days of my father Jared it came to pass that the children of men multiplied upon the face of the earth, and beautiful and comely daughters were born to them. While it was true that Jah-el and the holy angels were witnesses to the occurrences of the children of earth, they were not alone in their scrutiny. Satan and his host were also conscious. Some of the fallen angels of the dominion of Satan, those who would soon come to be known as the Evil Watchers, looked down from on high, with thoughts of exceeding wickedness.

Amongst the evil legions of Lucifer was a commanding angel whose name is Semjazael. In the days of my father Jared was he ruler over nine attending angels and commander of nineteen staff angels, these being rulers over nine attending angels, and together they were a force of two hundred. These are they who from high atop the mountain known as Hermon, from behind their cloaks of invisibility, took to the habit of lasciviously watching the daughters of men. It became their sport to view the intimacy of men with women, and in doing so became engulfed in a passion. They desired to share in what was meant only for the corporeal creation. They were of heaven, spiritual. What they were considering was abomination to its lowest degree. What macabre beings would such a union produce, flesh and angel? The children of men were soon to be made horridly aware.

It came to pass, in the days of my father Jared, before my birth, that Semjazael and his following decided to come upon the earth and live as men. Semjazael said to his command, "Let us go to the earth and put on flesh, and let us be gods amongst the people. Let us go and take the daughters of men as wives, as many as we see fit, and we shall lie down with them, and they shall bear us children." Semjazael continued by saying, "I fear that you may not agree to do this deed with me, and I alone shall have to pay the penalty of a great sin, therefore let us all swear an oath, and all bind ourselves by mutual imprecations not to abandon this plan, but carry it out." They swore all together to do as their leader suggested, and in all two hundred angels descended on the face of the earth. They descended at the base of the Mount of Hermon, and these are the names of the nineteen leaders; Arakibael, Rameel, Kokabiel, Tamiel, Ramiel, Danel, Ezeqeel, Baraqijel, Asael, Armarosel, Batarel, Ananel, Zaqiel, Samsapeel, Satarel, Turel, Jomjael, Sariel, and the sinister Azazel.

The fallen angels descended and materialized in the flesh, endowing themselves with genitals like those of horses. They took to themselves wives, as many as pleased them, and they began to defile themselves with them, and they taught them charms, and enchantments, and the working of roots, and made them acquainted with plants. The women of men became pregnant by the Evil Watchers, and they bore them great giants. They bore them sons and daughters of great height and strength, those who would become known as the Nephilim. Beings half human and half angel, and extremely cruel, they proceeded to consume all the acquisitions of men. These giants lorded over men, and placed them in grievous bondage, and the men of earth toiled to quench their insatiable appetites. It was impossible to do so, for these offspring were human only in form. These offspring of the unholy union of angel and flesh could not be satisfied, and soon there was nothing left in which to sustain them, so they began to turn against the animals of the earth, hunting them, killing them for sport, eating flesh, and drinking blood.

The Evil Watchers were intoxicated with the pleasures that their materialized flesh enabled them to feel. They instituted phallic worship, and caused the children of men to bow down before their exaggerated genitals. They instituted gross wantonness, fornication, and sodomy. Azazel taught men to make swords, knives, shields, and breastplates. He made known to the men of earth the different metals of the ground, and the art of working them. He taught men to make bracelets, and ornaments, and the use of antimony. He taught the children of earth to paint their eyelids, and all kinds of costly stones he made manifest and all coloring tinctures. Godlessness was rampant on the earth, men were led astray and made corrupt in all their ways. Semjazael taught enchantments and root cutting. Armorosel taught the resolving of enchantments. Baraqijel taught men astrology. Kokabiel taught the constellations, Araqiel the signs of the earth. Shamsiel taught the signs of the sun, and Sariel the signs of the moon. Men worshipped these god men, and men perished; they cried, and their cries went up to heaven.

Michael, Gabriel, Raphael, and Uriel looked down from on high and saw the abundance of blood being shed on the earth, and the lawlessness. They conversed one to another concerning these things saying, "The spilled blood of mankind cries out from the earth up to the gates of heaven, and the souls of men are crying to we the holy ones of heaven that we bring their cause before the Most High."

Michael requested an audience before the throne of Jah-el for himself and his brethren of the throne platform. Jah-el consented, and they took their audience positions around the throne. They spoke in one accord, "Lord of lords, God of gods, King of kings, and God of the ages, You have made all things. You see all things. You see that Azazel has taught all unrighteousness on earth and revealed the eternal secrets which were preserved in heaven, which men were striving to learn, and Semjazael whom You have given authority to bear rule over his associates. They have gone to the daughters of men on the earth, and have lain with them, and have defiled themselves, and revealed to them all manners of sin. The women have borne giants, and the whole earth is filled with bloodshed and unrighteousness. Behold the souls of those who have died how they wail and make suit to the gates of heaven, and their lamentation has ascended and cannot cease, because of the lawless deeds which are taking place in the earth. Lord Jah-el You see all things, and You suffer them, and You do not say to us what we are to do to them in regard these things." The Lord Jah-el remained mute for a great long while, and then in a voice of assured consolation said, "All things in My own time."

When my father Jared was one hundred and sixty years of age, and my forefather Adam six hundred and twenty, he took to wife my mother Baraka, the daughter of Rasujal, a daughter of his father's brother. When my father Jared was one hundred and sixty-two years of age, and my forefather Adam six hundred and twenty-two, I was born. I am Enoch. I am the first son of the seventh generation from my forefather Adam.

I am the teller of this story, the history of man. I saw the vision of the Holy One seated in Heaven which the angels showed me, and from them I heard everything, and from them I understood as I saw, though not for my generation, but for a remote one which was far to come—your generation.

Before my birth, and after, we that were considered righteous in the earth avoided the cities of men, for in them was found every sort of wickedness. We avoided the lands inhabited by the gigantic offspring of the Evil Watchers and we dwelt close to the Garden of Paradise in proximity to the reminder of Jah-el, the two guarding cherubim with the flaming sword. The world was far removed from us, for Adam our forefather had spoken to us the promise that Jah-el had made to him. He would insistently warn, "Stay clear of sin, that the Lord Jah-el will remember you on the day of resurrection."

In the sixty-fourth year of my existence, and the six hundred and eighty-sixth of my aged forefather Adam, I took to wife Edni, the daughter of Danel, the daughter of my father's brother, and I was the first among men to learn to write, for it was the will of Jah-el. In the sixty-fifth year of my life, and the six hundredth and eighty-seventh year of my forefather Adam, did Edni bear me a son, and I called his name Methuselah. It was twelve years after the birth of my son that the voice of Jah-el came to me in a dream vision, and Jah-el said, "Enoch, you have found favor in My sight and I have set forth a task that you shall do. Arise from your sleep, and bring nothing but your instruments of writing. Tell no one of your going for I shall lead you to a place of My choosing, one remote and obscure."

Upon my waking I lifted myself from my bed, and behold standing at the entrance of my cave a bright one from heaven. He said to me, "Enoch I am Gabriel, one of the holy angels, and it is my duty to lead you to the place of your residence." Gabriel led me to a large lake, in a land called Dan, to the south and west of the mountain called Hermon. I was hidden and not one of the children of men knew where I was concealed, or where I abode, or what had become of me, and my activities had to do with the Evil Watchers, and my days were spent consulting with the holy ones.

The Evil Watchers had grown weary of their stay on earth. They had indulged themselves to capacity. Semjazael called his force together. It was time to leave. It was their intention to return to their dark lord Lucifer and his kingdom of gloom. The two hundred god men gathered at the base of Hermon, preparing to shed their earthly bodies and return to the spirit. They were introduced to a shocking revelation. They found that they could not revert. Jah-el had relinquished their right to ever return to the freedom of heaven, even if it was one far below the third one. Semjazael and his host were earthbound. They unashamedly began to pray, and make entreaty to Jah-el, but found it impossible to lift their heads toward heaven. Panic permeated the small band. Jah-el's time of recompense was at hand.

In the seventy-seventh year of my existence on the face of the earth, did the Lord Jah-el summon me. I, Enoch, was giving praise to the Lord of majesty, the King of the ages, at the place of His choosing. I was hidden, and without warning the angel Gabriel appeared before me saying, "Enoch, you scribe of righteousness, go and declare to the Evil Watchers who have left their station, and have defiled themselves, and have acted as the children of men, and have taken themselves wives. Say to them, this is the decree of the Lord Jah-el. You have brought great destruction upon the earth, and you shall have neither peace nor forgiveness of your sins. Inasmuch as you have come to find great delight in your vile offspring, the murder of your beloved ones you shall see. Over the destruction of your children shall you cry out in great pain, and you shall make supplication to me unto eternity but mercy and peace shall you not attain."

I went to the place of the Evil Watchers, and found them at the base of mount Hermon. I told them all that Jah-el had commanded me. I told them the word of the Lord of hosts. The one that is named Azazel came forward and began to entreat me saying, "Surely Jah-el will have mercy upon us and our children, for they are precious to us. Make entreaty to Him on our behalf, that they should live and that we be allowed to return to our rightful place." I stood and took in the sight before me. "An angel of the Most High," I thought to myself, "how could such a one have fallen from such heights?" I returned the words of the Lord of spirits to the evil one before me. I answered him saying, "Azazel, you shall have no peace. A severe sentence has gone forth from the mouth of Jah-el, and you are to be put into bonds. You shall not have any of your requests granted because of your unrighteousness, and because of your teaching the children of men all the ways of ungodliness." Then I spoke to the entire assembly the remainder of what I was commissioned to say, and they were afraid. Fear and trembling seized them and they besought me to write a letter of petition for them that they might find forgiveness, and they beseeched me to make intercession for them before the Lord of ages. I wrote out their pleas and their prayers in regard to their deeds individually, and in regard their requests that they might attain the forgiveness of the Lord of hosts. I returned to the place from which I had journeyed, the place in the land of Dan, the place by the lake. There I made entreaty before the Lord Jah-el. I read over and over in repetition the petition of the Evil Watchers until I fell asleep. And behold a dream came to me, and visions fell upon me. I saw visions of chastisement, and a voice bidding me to tell all to the Evil Watchers and reprimand them.

When I awoke I returned to them at their dwelling at the base of the mount called Hermon. They were gathered together at the place called Abelsjail, which is between Lebanon and Hermon, weeping with their faces covered in their hands. I approached them and recounted to them all the visions I had seen in my sleep, and I began to speak the words of righteousness and to reprimand the Evil Watchers saying,

"I saw in my sleep what I am now to say with my tongue of flesh, and with the breath of my mouth, which the Great One has given to men to converse therewith, and understand with the heart. As He has created and given to man the power of understanding the word of wisdom so has He created me also, and given me the power to reprimand you. I wrote out your petition and in my vision it appeared thus, that your petition will not be granted to you throughout all the days of eternity. Your judgment is fixed. From henceforward you shall not ascend into heaven, no never unto all eternity. It has been decreed by the Lord Jah-el that you are to be bound, but before your ending you shall witness the complete destruction of all your children and they shall fall before you by the sword. Your petition on their behalf shall not be granted, nor your own, even though you weep and pray, and speak all the words contained in the writing which I have written, and now am I to relate to you the vision which I received from the Lord Jah-el."

The Evil Watchers sat before me, eyes staring blankly. Some of them broke forth in loud wails. Semjazael, Azazel, and Kokabiel motioned to the others to desist their caterwauling. The three strode forward to the head of the assembly, Azazel always the one most vocal. He stationed himself before me, focusing his evil gaze, pinpointing the centers of my eyes. His speech disgusting, his manner oozing depravity, he sat down before me, legs crossed. Of all the Evil Watchers Azazel was the most sinister, his defiance an obsession, his air putrid. He snapped an order to me hissing, "Continue scribe, tell us our fate." With all the vileness before me still was I struck with pity. They would soon come to know the wrath I was shown. As merciful as the Lord is to those who are in His favor, He is as merciless to those who are not. These angels before me were not in the favor of the Lord of hosts, and they would pay for their defiance for all eternity. I continued saying,

"When I was asleep great distress came upon me, and I was weeping in my sleep. I could not understand what this distress was, or what was happening to me. Then there appeared before me two men, extremely big, their faces shining like the sun, and their eyes like burning lights. I arose from my sleep and saw clearly these two men before me. I was afraid and terror took hold of me, and the men said to me, Have courage Enoch, do not fear, the eternal God has sent us to you. They placed me between themselves, and lifted me aloft by means of their great wings. They bore me through the first heaven, through the ether, and into a vast expanse. Below me they showed me a very great sea, a sea that engulfed the entire earth, and it stretched as far as the eye could see, and I marveled. Through the vast expanse, of what I came to know as the second heaven, we traveled at a speed staggering to the imagination. We soon arrived at an entrance, an immense portal at the end of our journey governed by seven archangels and a flaming sword. Upon gaining entry through this portal, we approached a wall built of what appeared to be crystal pulsating like flaming fire. We flew through the great gates of the great wall. The gates were posted by angels of great height, of the order cherub, one to the left side, and one to the right. We drew nigh to a structure of colossal proportion, whose walls appeared as tasseled crystals and the groundwork the same.

As we entered this structure I cast my gaze to the ceiling above, and the ceiling shone like the paths of lightning and of shooting stars. The walls flickered as if engulfed in the flames of fire, and the many entrances glowed in effervescent luminosity. My fear was surpassed only by my mesmerization of what I was seeing. Then we drew nearer to a second house, one so vast that my eyes could not encompass its length, breadth, or its height. A very great and immense doorway opened before us, and the mighty wings of my bearers propelled us through it easily. This house appeared to be constructed of great columns of fire, and in every respect it excelled in splendor and magnificence. I cannot begin to describe to you its beauty and the wonders that stood before me. The floor of this house was of what appeared to be flaming fire, but it burned not. It appeared as a great flickering sea. As we entered into this house I looked to the ceiling, and the vastness was as such as when I was here on earth gazing heavenward. In its ceiling were lightning and the paths of shooting stars. My attention was snatched toward what appeared to be singing. I peered forward and beheld a lofty expanse, its appearance as crystal, suspended above great golden wheels shining as the sun.

The two men with me lifted me up even higher and I saw a very great light, and fiery troops of great archangels, incorporeal forces and dominions, orders and governments, cherubim, seraphim, and ophanim. I became increasingly afraid and began to tremble with terror, and the two men said to me, Have courage Enoch, do not fear. They showed me the Lord Jah-el from afar, sitting on His very high throne. From underneath the throne came streams of flaming fire, and I found it impossible to look thereon.

The Great Jah-el sat upon His throne, and His raiment shone more brightly than the sun and was whiter than the purest alabaster. None of the angels could enter and behold His face, by reason of His magnificence and glory. The flaming fire was round about Him, and a great fire stood before Him, and none could draw nigh to Him. Ten thousand times ten thousand stood before Him, yet He needed no counselor. These holy ones who were close to Him did not leave from before His presence, nor depart from Him. All of the heavenly troops came and stood according to their rank, and bowed before the Lord, and then went to their places in joy and felicity, singing songs in the boundless light with small and tender voices, gloriously serving Him.

The cherubim and seraphim standing about the throne of Jah-el, the six-winged and many-eyed ones did not depart. They stood before the Lord's face doing His will, and covering the entirety of the throne platform singing with gentle voices before the Lord's face, saying Holy. Holy. Holy. Lord Ruler. Heaven and earth are full of your glory. When I had seen these things the two with me said to me, Enoch, thus far it is commanded for us to journey with you. They took their leave, but before their departure they placed me upon the throne platform of the Lord. They placed me upon a cloth of immeasurable beauty that served as a barrier between my feet and the surface of the chariot expanse. I was before the throne of God Himself, but surrounded from His view by the many-eyed ones standing before His throne. I was encircled. I was alone, and I became exceedingly afraid almost to the point of convulsion. I fell on my face and began to cry out to myself, Oh woe is me, what has befallen me? The Lord Jah-el summoned one of His archangels, and sent him to me. He approached and spoke to me the message of the Lord saying, Have courage Enoch, do not fear, arise before the Lord's face. Arise, and come with me. I answered Him saying, My lord, my life is almost departed from me because of terror and trembling. I called to the two who had brought me to this place. I pleaded with the Lord that He would restore to me the angels with whom I had come. I was familiar with these two, and on these two I had come to rely. The Lord answered my prayer, and before me stood the angel named Gabriel and he that is named Uriel.

Gabriel caught me up as a leaf caught up by the wind, and placed me closer before the Lord. From there I saw the appearance of the Lord's face like iron made to glow in fire and brought out emitting sparks, and it burns. I saw the Lord's face and it is ineffable, marvelous, and awesome to look upon. Who am I to tell you of the Lord's unspeakable being, and of His very wonderful face? I cannot tell the quantity of His many instructions and various edicts, nor the quantity of those standing round Him, nor their unceasing singing, nor His immutable beauty, greatness, and glory. I fell prone and bowed before the Lord, and He said to me, have courage Enoch, do not fear. Arise and stand before My face. Then there appeared one before me mightier than all the angels of heaven, one rugged and a possessor of great strength. The Lord Jah-el smiled at this one as he approached. This one is the archangel who is named Michael, of the order cherub.

Upon receiving his instruction from the Lord of hosts, Michael lifted me up and stationed me even closer before the Lord's face. Then the Lord Jah-el spoke saying, Let Enoch stand before me. And the glorious ones bowed down to Him and said, Let Enoch do according to Your word. The Lord Jah-el then instructed, Michael take Enoch out of his earthly garments, and anoint him with My sweet ointment, and put him into the garments of My glory. Michael did as Jah-el commanded. He anointed me, and dressed me, and the appearance of the ointment is as the light of the shining sun, it's smell mild like sweet morning dew. I looked at myself and to my utter astonishment, I had become like one of the glorious ones.

Afterwards did Michael bring me directly before the face of the Lord. Without fore thought I immediately prostrated myself before the Lord of spirits, and the Lord called me with His own mouth and said to me, Come forth Enoch and hear My words. Michael bade me to rise and approach the Lord of hosts, and I did so with my head bowed low. The Lord Jah-el then continued His conversing with me and said, Fear not Enoch, you righteous man and scribe of righteousness. Come closer and hear My voice. Go say this to the Evil Watchers who have sent you to make intercession for them. Say to them, thus is the decree of the Lord Jah-el. You should intercede for men and not men for you. Why have you left your proper station and lain with the daughters of men and defiled yourselves, and taken yourselves wives, and done like the children of men and begotten giants as your sons? You were once holy, spiritual, living the eternal life. You have defiled yourselves with the blood of women and have begotten children with the blood of flesh, and as the children of men have lusted after flesh. Therefore shall I give your sons the desire to take wives of the females born to you, and they shall impregnate them and beget children by them, and they shall destroy one another. You were formerly spiritual, living the eternal life; immortal for all the generations of the world. It was not appointed that wives should be given to you, for you are spiritual and in heaven is your dwelling. Because you have perpetrated this gross error in bonds shall you be placed for all eternity, but first shall you see the slaughter of your beloved ones. There shall be great and complete destruction amongst them. When they are killed one by the other then shall evil spirits proceed from their corpses, because they are born of the union of angel and flesh. They shall become evil spirits in the earth, and evil spirits shall they be called. As for the spirits of heaven in the heavens shall be their dwelling place, but as for the spirits born upon the earth on the earth shall they reside. The spirits that arise from the corpses of the giants shall afflict, oppress, destroy, attack, wage war, and work destruction upon the earth, and cause great calamity. These spirits will have no need of food and drink yet will they hunger and thirst, and desire to cause offence. These spirits shall go forth from the corpses of your dead children and shall inhabit the children of men, as many as they may possess, because from bodies they have proceeded, and to inhabit bodies is their desire. From the days of slaughter and destruction and death of your offspring; from the souls of whose flesh the spirits having gone forth shall destroy without incurring judgment, thus shall they destroy until the day of consummation, the great judgment in which the age shall be consummated over you Evil Watchers and the godless. Now to the fallen minions who have sent you to intercede for them, who have been aforetime in heaven, say to them, You have been in heaven but all of the mysteries had not been revealed to you. You knew worthless ones and these in the error of your ways have made known to the women, and through these mysteries women and men work much evil on the earth. Say to them, this is the decree of the Lord God Jah-el. You shall have no peace.

Jah-el turned His attention from me and with His voice summoned Gabriel and Uriel and said to them, Gabriel, Uriel, take the man Enoch and make known to him the destiny of the Evil Watchers. The two angels with whom I had journeyed so far lifted me aloft and sped me to a location in the northern part of the kingdom of heaven. They sat me down at the edge of a deep abyss with great columns of heavenly fire and among them I saw columns of fire fall which were beyond measure in height and depth. Beyond the abyss I saw a place which had no firmament of heaven above, and no firmly founded earth beneath it. There was no water to be found there, but it was a waste and horrible place. I gazed fixated into this place and beheld imprisoned therein one hundred and ninety-five stars like great burning mountains, and to me when I inquired regarding them the angel Uriel said, This place is the end of heaven and earth, and will serve as the prison for the stars of the host of heaven who have transgressed the commandment of the Lord. Here shall stand the angels who have connected themselves with women whose spirits are assuming many forms, defiling mankind and leading them astray into sacrificing to demons as gods. Here shall they be imprisoned until the day of the Great Judgment in which they shall be judged.

Then the angels that were my escort lifted me once more and brought me to another place, this one more horrible than the former. I looked and perceived a fearful sight; a great fire which burned and blazed, the place was cleft as far as the abyss, being full of great descending columns of fire, neither its extent or magnitude could I conjecture. There were all sorts of cruel tortures in this place, pitch black darkness and gloom. There was no light, but murky fire constantly flamed aloft. There was in the midst of this place a fiery river flowing, everywhere fire, and all about weapons of sadistic torture. I turned to my companions, awed at the sight before me. Then I said, How fearful this place is and terrible to look upon. Uriel looked into my eyes, his body reflecting as a glowing coal the fire of that place, and asked me, Enoch, why have you such fear and why are you frightened of this place? Be not afraid for this place is the final destination of all fallen angels, demons, and eternal spirits of wicked mankind. This place is prepared for all who dishonor the Lord Jah-el, who on earth practice sin against nature, and who know not their Creator, and bow down before soulless, lifeless gods, who cannot see nor hear. Vain gods. For these is this place prepared for their everlasting inheritance, after the great and final judgment."

As soon as I did conclude the message of Jah-el to the Evil Watchers did they want to destroy me, but the hand of Jah-el protected me and I returned to the waters of Dan. At my return the angel Gabriel met me and said to me, "Enoch, you scribe of righteousness, the Lord has decreed that you shall return to your place amongst the children of men, and say to your father and your father's fathers all that you have seen. Say to them that the Lord Jah-el is seated upon His throne, and all things shall occur in His own time. Go now Enoch, and live until the Lord summons you once more." With that the angel Gabriel disappeared from before my face and I returned to the people of my dwelling, to my wife, and my child, and I made known to them all that the Lord had shown me.

When I was two hundred and fifty years of age, and my forefather Adam eight hundred and seventy-two, my son Methuselah took to wife Edna, the daughter of my brother Azrial. In the two hundred and fifty-second year of my existence, the eight hundred and seventy-fourth of my aged forefather Adam, and the one hundredth eighty-seventh of my son Methuselah, did his wife Edna bear him a son, and he called his name Lamech. One hundred and seventy-five years had elapsed since my calling from the Lord, and the children of men had waxed even deeper into iniquity. The Evil Watchers were wrecking havoc with insane vengeance. Led by Azazel, Semjazael, and the now infamous Kokabiel, the Evil Watchers developed greater depths of depravity. Already the decree of Jah-el was coming to pass. The sons of the Evil Watchers had begun to marry their sisters, and produce offspring of their own. The giants became divided into three classes. First there were the Nephilim, who were birthed from the unnatural mixture of angel and flesh. Then these ones intermarried, and birthed the Eljo. In turn, the Eljo intermarried and birthed the Eluid. As their numbers increased and the clans thereof, they began to hate one another. The Evil Watchers could do nothing but watch the prophecy of Jah-el unfold before them, and as they witnessed it vented their frustrations on the children of men.

The earth was wicked and corrupt. It was a time of sorcerers, witches, wizards, and giants. The people were drunkards and users of strange brews, potions, and plants. Gross fornications and adulteries of every sort were rampant, men lying with men and women with women; orgies, bestiality, and the working of every detestable thing before the Lord of hosts. The people were idolaters, worshipping idols and men. They were worshippers of human genitals, and sacrificed their children in the fire. The Evil Watchers had come to earth to indulge in the pleasures of the flesh, and in so doing had opened to mankind every sort of wickedness imaginable. They were sadistic, and took great joy in inflicting pain for sport. They howled with laughter as their sons skewered men, roasting them over open flame and eating their flesh. They hunted men as animals, and took whatever they desired, and the most-wicked of men allied themselves with them. They hunted the great beasts of the earth, those that in your time are known as dinosaurs, and the great beasts fled to the extremities of the earth, and their fear of man became great.

CHAPTER 6

NATURAL DEATH

Time progressed upon the earth, and while the earth did not seem to erode with age man did. It was the concern of us all—the increasing decline of the health of our now skin-wrinkled, white-haired, aged fore-parents. Father Adam and Mother Eve seemed to wane in strength with each passing day. Still even more difficult to bear were the many infirmities they suffered. Of all the offspring of our forefather Adam, Seth was of the most concern. He was the favorite of his mother, and though he was also advanced in years he catered hand and foot to his aged parents.

In the three hundred and eighth year of my existence on the face of the earth, and the nine hundred and thirtieth of our aged forefather Adam, did he fall sick, and he cried out in a loud voice saying, "Let all my sons come to me that I may see them before I die." We gathered ourselves at the place in which the patriarch dwelled, I and Edni, my son Methuselah and his wife Edna, Lamech, my father Jared, my mother Baraka, Mahalalel and Dinah, Cainan and Maulaleth, Enos and Naom, Seth and Azura, and all the offspring from our aged fore parents who were separated to the worship of the Lord Jah-el. Mother Eve had prepared a pallet on the ground, and was dabbing the face of her husband with cool water in an attempt to ease his discomfort. We gathered around, the eldest toward the middle, and Seth at his father's side. Adam said to Seth,

"Hear my son Seth, that I may relate to you what I heard and saw after your mother and I were cast from Paradise. When we were at prayer there came to me Michael the archangel, one of the holy ones of heaven, a messenger of God. And I saw a chariot like the wind, and its wheels were fiery, and I was caught up into the paradise of righteousness. I saw the Lord Jah-el sitting, and His face was flaming fire that could not be endured. Many thousands of angels were round about Him. When I saw this I was confused and terror seized me, and I bowed myself low before Him. Jah-el spoke to me and said, Adam, your time of death is near because you did transgress My commandment. You chose to listen to the voice of your wife. I gave you the power to hold her to your will and you exercised it not. When I heard these words I stretched forth flat on the earth and said, My Lord, all powerful and merciful God, Holy and Righteous One, please do not blot out my name from Your memory, for I am about to die, and my breath is about to go out of my mouth. Please Lord God, do not banish me from You forever. After I said these things then the Lord said to me, Since the time that I created you, you have been created with a love of knowledge. Because of this, I shall not take away from your offspring the right to serve Me. When I heard these things, I gave ever-increasing praise to the Lord and proclaimed, You Lord Jah-el are the true light gleaming above all lights. You are the living life, the infinite mighty power. You have bestowed upon the race of men the abundance of Your mercy. After I had worshipped the Lord, Michael seized my hand, and cast me from the paradise of vision. Michael held in his hand a rod and with it he touched the water surrounding Paradise and the water became as crystal, hard to the touch. He escorted me across the water, and brought me back to the place from which I was taken. Listen to me my son as I make known to you all of the secrets which were revealed to me, by my eating of the forbidden tree. This is what will occur in the age of men, and these are the intentions of the Lord God concerning the race of men. The Lord will appear in a flame of fire, and a two-edged sword shall protrude from His mouth. From His mouth will He utter commandments and statutes and they shall sanctify Him in the house of His habitation, and He will show them the marvelous place of His majesty. They shall build a house to the Lord Jah-el, in a land He has prepared for them. They shall be a headstrong people, and they will transgress His laws, and their sanctuary will be burned, and their land deserted, and the people dispersed. Twice shall this occur, but once more will Jah-el cause them to be re-gathered and again they shall build the house of God, and in the last the house of God shall be exalted greater than of old, then once more will iniquity exceed righteousness. Then Jah-el will dwell with men on earth and righteousness will begin to shine. The house of God will be honored, and their enemies will no longer be able to hurt they who believe in God. Jah-el will stir up for Himself a faithful people, whom He shall save for all eternity, and the impious shall be punished.

Heaven and earth, night and day, and all creatures
shall obey Him. He shall repel from Himself all the
wicked, and they shall be condemned. Happy is the
man who has ruled his soul when the judgment shall
come to pass, and the greatness of Jah-el be seen
among men, and their deeds inquired into by Him,
the just Judge."

After Adam said these things to his son, he broke forth
in awful groaning saying, "My sons, I am sick with pain."
And all said to him, "What does it mean Father, this illness
and pain?" Then Seth said to Adam, "Father, perhaps you
are desiring the fruit of Paradise. Tell me and I will go to the
nearest gate of Eden, and I will place dust upon my head,
and throw myself down on the ground, and lament and make
entreaty to the Lord on your behalf. Perhaps He will hear
me, and send His angel to bring me the fruit."

Adam answered and said, "No my son I do not long for
the fruit, but I feel weakness and great pain in my body."
Seth answered, "What is this suffering my father, hide it not
from us but please tell us what it is." Adam looked towards
his son's face gazing down on him, bewilderment etched
across Seth's searching eyes. Adam gripped tighter his son's
hand and began saying,

"When the Lord Jah-el made us, me and your
mother, He gave us power to eat of every tree which
is in Paradise, but concerning one only He charged us
not to eat. It is because of this disobedience that I die.
When we were in the Garden we were guarded by the
angels of Jah-el and the hour drew nigh for the angels
that were guarding your mother to go up and worship
before the throne. I was far from her and the enemy
knew that she was alone and deceived her, and gave

her of the forbidden fruit. Then she gave also to me and I did eat. The Lord was extremely angered with us and He came to Paradise and called us forth in a voice great and terrible, and there He cursed us. He said to me, Adam, because you have broken My commandment, I have brought upon your body seventy-two strokes. The trouble of the first stroke is the pain of the eyes. The affliction of the second stroke is of the hearing, and likewise in turn shall all of the strokes against your flesh befall you."

As Adam said this to his son, he clutched his chest and moaned, "What shall I do? I am in great distress." Eve wept and said, "Adam rise up and give me half of your trouble, and I shall endure it, for it is on my account that you suffer." Adam exhaled a long burdened sigh, his agony finally convincing him to desperation, and said to his wife, "Eve arise and go with our son Seth near to Paradise, and place dirt upon your heads, and weep, and pray before the Lord. Ask Him to have mercy on me, and send His angel to Paradise, and give me of the tree out of which the oil flows, and bring it to me that I should anoint myself, and cure this ailment."

Seth and Eve arose and went toward the direction of Paradise. Seth being the faster ran ahead of his mother. When Eve finally caught up with him she saw her son being assailed by a wild beast, a cotur. Eve screeched at the beast, her arms flailing and screamed, "You wicked cat, how dare you to fight against the image of God. How is it that your mouth is opened against him? Why have you not called to mind your subjection?" As Eve shouted these things, she knew full well the answers. How had her mouth opened to eat of the tree in which Jah-el had commanded her not to eat? On this account had the very earth fallen into imperfection, and the beasts of the earth were no longer under the subjection of man. As the cotur darted into the cover of the jungle, Seth shouted defiantly, "Close your mouth against the image of God, and do not attack me again from this day forward until the Day of Judgment."

Eve and Seth arrived at the gate of Paradise, and forthwith they began making entreaty to the Lord of hosts. Then the Lord Jah-el sent Michael, and Michael said to Seth, "Man of God, do not weary yourself with prayers and entreaties concerning the tree of life for your father shall not have it now, but at the end of time. Then will all flesh be raised up, from your father Adam till that great day, all that shall be of the holy people. Then shall the delights of paradise be given to them, and the Lord will be in their midst. They will no longer sin before His face, for the evil heart shall be taken away from them. There shall be given to them in return a heart understanding only the good, and to serve God for eternity. Go back to your father, for the term of his life has been fulfilled, and in three days' time shall he die. When his soul is departing, you shall behold the scene of his passing." Michael then made his departure from them, and Eve and Seth returned to Adam and told him all that the archangel had said. With that Adam gazed up at his wife and in a voice projecting blame said, "Eve, Eve, What have you caused in us? You have brought upon us death, and it is lording over all our children." Then Adam demanded his wife to tell us all the manner of her sin.

When Eve had relayed to us all that was in her heart, she said, "Now then my children, I have made known to you the way in which I was deceived. Be careful in your lives that you transgress not against the good." When Eve had said this in the midst of us, while Adam was lying before us tormented by his pain, Eve questioned him in a voice of wonderment saying, "How is it that you are dying and I live on? How much longer will I have to live after your death?" Adam answered without opening his pain-clenched eyes and said, "Think not concerning it Eve, for you are soon to follow." Then he continued, "When I die, anoint me with oil and let no man touch me further until the angel of the Lord shall give instruction concerning me. For God will not forget me. Now arise, and go and pray until my spirit is given into the hands of He who gave it. Pray concerning me for we know not how we shall meet our Maker, whether He be angry with us or merciful and intend to have pity on us and receive us."

On the third day Eve rose from the shelter built for Adam in his sickness, went outside, and fell to the ground and began to lament, "I have sinned O God. I have sinned O God of all. I have sinned against You." While she was praying these words the angel of humanity, Michael, appeared before her and raised her up and said, "Arise Eve, for behold your husband Adam has gone out from his body. Arise, and behold his spirit borne aloft to meet his Maker." Eve rose up and wiped away her tears with her hands. The angel said to her, "Lift up your eyes and see." Eve gazed steadfastly into heaven and again she saw Jah-el's chariot of light borne by four bright angels. It was impossible for any born of women to tell of the glory of those that bore the chariot. When they came to the place where the spirit of Adam was they halted; the chariot and the seraphim. She saw a golden censer placed between the chariot and the spirit of Adam, and all the angels with censers and frankincense came in haste to the incense offering and blew it and the smoke veiled the sky. Then the angels fell down and worshipped Jah-el, crying aloud, "Jah-el, Holy One, have pardon for he is Your image, and the work of Your holy hands."

Eve beheld two great and fearful wonders standing in the presence of God, and she cried aloud to Seth and said, "Seth, come forth from the body of your father. Come to me, and you shall see a spectacle." Seth came forth from the hut of his parents, and upon seeing his mother asked, "What is the trouble, why are you weeping?" Eve replied, "Look up and see with your eyes the heavens opened, and see how the spirit of your father lies on its face, and all the holy angels praying on his behalf saying, Please Lord Jah-el pardon him Father of all, for he is Your image." The angels that were lying on their faces stood, and cried aloud in voices like trumpet blasts saying, "Blessed be the glory of the Lord and the works of His making. He has pitied Adam, the creature of His hands." When the angels had said these words there came forth one of the seraphim, and he took the spirit of Adam and washed him three times in the lake known as Acherusian. Then the Lord Jah-el said, "Adam, what have you done? If you had only kept My commandment, there would be no joy in the domain of he that is called Satan. Yet I say to you, I will transform you again to your former glory. I will set you upon the throne of your deceiver. He shall be cast into a place that I have reserved for him, but first shall he see you in his place. Then shall he be condemned, he and all that followed him. He shall be grieved throughout eternity when he sees you sitting at the position that was once his."

Jah-el permitted Adam to lie before Him for three hours. Thereafter the Lord of hosts stretched forth His hand and took Adam, and placed him in the care of Michael. Michael took Adam and left him in the holding place of saints.

After all this, the angels asked concerning the laying out of the remains. Jah-el commanded that the angels should assemble in His presence, each in his order, and all the angels did so. Then the Lord of hosts approached us. He came forth mounted on the four winds with all the hosts of heaven, some with censers and others with golden trumpets and all settled in the Garden of Eden. The throne chariot of the Lord landed, and rested over the tree of life. As the hosts of heaven approached their point of touchdown all of the fragrant flowers of Paradise were stirred and the intoxicating aroma caused us all to fall into a deep sleep, all save for Seth because he was born according to the appointment of God. Adam's body lay there on the earth, and Seth grieved over his father. Jah-el spoke to the archangels Michael, Gabriel, Raphael, and Uriel and said, "Go into Paradise and bring back oil of the oil of fragrance and pour it on his body." The angels did as Jah-el commanded, and upon their return busied themselves in preparing Adam's body for burial. Then Jah-el said, "Let the body of Abel also be brought for he is unburied since the day Cain killed him, for wicked Cain took great pains to conceal him but could not for the earth would not receive him."

Both Adam and Abel his son were buried in the earth, by the instructions of Jah-el. They were buried in the very same place from which Jah-el had taken the dust to form him. Jah-el sent seven angels throughout Eden and they brought back many fragrant spices, and placed them in the graves. Then the Lord said, "From dust you were taken and to dust you shall return."

With Adam's burial complete, Jah-el turned His attention to Seth and said, "Seth you alone have witnessed the burial place of your father. Speak not its location to any for I forbid it." Seth fell to the ground, and lay prostrate before the Lord of spirits, and replied, "I shall obey Your word Lord God. My mouth is sealed."

Jah-el summoned His forces, but unlike His coming to earth His angels did not precede His departure. Seth stood gazing at the throne chariot. How immense it was in its proportion of sitting over the Garden of Paradise. Seth stood astonished as the cherubim of the four wheels began beating their mighty wings, first slowly as the beatings of whooping cranes as they prepare for flight. Then without warning the wings of the cherubim changed to the pitch of a humming-bird, then to that of a bee. They beat at such a speed that Seth could no longer see them, and the four cherubim of the wheels appeared as though they were men fixed upon nothing in the center of the wheels. The sound was as no sound that Seth could describe, and the winds created by their beating wings sent the greenery of Paradise violently lashing to and fro.

First the chariot of Jah-el moved ever so slightly, then without warning it lifted upwards, moved backwards, then sideways to the right. It moved with the mechanical quickness as is the flight of a hovering dragonfly, as if to align itself in some proper co-ordinates. Jah-el's leaving earth was of such swiftness that Seth could not determine His departure; for in one second the chariot of Jah-el was then it was not. All of the billions of angels that had come to earth with God followed His departure, and their departure was as lightning moves from earth to sky. As they departed they sang songs of praise, the spectacle of such was indescribable and witnessed only by Seth.

As the final angel ascended there was created a vortex, and the syrupy sweetness of the flowers was vacuumed away from the earth. In a short space of time we began to awaken, and Seth began to relay to us all that he saw. We sat before him trancelike, our attention clinging to each syllable that came from his mouth.

Six days after Adam's death, Eve perceived that she too was about to die. She assembled all her sons and daughters, and said, "Hear me my children. I will tell you what the archangel Michael said to your father and I after our ousting from Paradise, that because of our transgressing the law of Jah-el the Lord God would bring upon our race the anger of His judgment. First by water, the second by fire. By these two will the Lord judge the whole human race. So hearken to my instruction. Make both tablets of stone and of clay. Write on them all that you have seen and heard from us. Then if by water the Lord judge our race, the tablets of clay will dissolve and the tablets of stone will remain. If by fire the tablets of stone will be broken, and the tablets of clay will be baked hard."

Eve's health deteriorated speedily before our eyes. She grieved and wept bitterly concerning her husband's passing into death. But the thing that tortured her most was that she knew not where he was buried for when the Lord buried Adam she was asleep, she and all we offspring save for Seth. It was the decree of Jah-el that Adam's burial place be unknown, that we would not cause it to become a shrine and a place of sorrow. Eve prayed earnestly in the hour of her death, that she too would be buried in the same place as her husband. After Eve had prayed she gazed heavenward, and groaned aloud, and smote her breasts, and said, "God of all, receive my spirit." And straightway she delivered up her spirit to the holding place of the Lord Jah-el.

Michael was dispatched to earth and taught Seth how to prepare his mother for burial. Then Michael and the three angels that accompanied him took Eve's body and buried it in the place where Adam and Abel were. Thereafter, Michael spoke to Seth with these instructions, "Lay out in this wise every man that dies, till the day of the resurrection." After giving him this rule Michael continued, "Mourn not beyond six days but on the seventh rest, and rejoice in it, because on the seventh day God rejoices, and we angels also for the soul that has passed from Earth in His favor awaits Him in paradise." Then the four angels glorified God, saying, "Holy. Holy. Holy, is the Lord God Jah-el. Heaven and earth are full of His glory." With that praise completed, the angels lifted themselves from the earth's surface to return from whence they had come.

Seth, myself, and all of our family who maintained the laws of Jah-el, stood motionless for a great long while, heads tilted upward toward the direction in which the angels of Jah-el had ascended. Some wept openly, while others wailed hysterically of the events that had transpired in such a short period of time. They were no more, they were gone, our primary parents, our most ancient elders, our link to what was. We who remained were initiated into still yet another outcome of our parent's transgression, that being the helpless sensation of total despair.

We followed the instructions of Michael and on the seventh day rejoiced, finding comfort in his words. Surely our aged fore bearers were now free. No sickness, no pain of agedness, no adversary anymore. Such an unnatural occurrence as death was now natural to man, and men were dying in abundance. While we who were godly could look forward to length of life it was not so for the ungodly, for murder and human sacrifice were practiced amongst them. The offspring of the Evil Watchers were at war with one another, and the bloodletting was of hideous proportion. The stench of ungodliness kept us distant from those who lived lives of wantonness and debauchery. While our own stench of inherent sin kept us from entering Eden, the cherubim of the Garden's entrance and the flaming sword of the Spirit a constant reminder.

As darkness draped the seventh day I lay awake in our place of abode, our fire's light casting dancing shadows on the walls and ceiling. I inhaled the aromas of my life, playing a game of holding them in and trying not to let them go. I listened to my wife Edni sleeping beside me. I perused the events of the past twelve days, and the jubilation of this day. I thought of the Lord God Jah-el, and all that I was shown concerning the Evil Watchers. For some inexplicable reason, a reason that surely escaped my own understanding, I was chosen. Called of Him. How mystical and amazing were these times of my dwelling on the Earth. It was in this fit of wonderment and perplexity, my mind formulating thoughts at the speed of a cherub's travel, that I finally succumbed to sleep, gentle, restful, and peaceful sleep.

CHAPTER 7

THE TRANSLATION

After one years passing from the death of our father Adam, I being three hundred nine years of age, my son Methuselah two hundred forty-four and young Lamech fifty-seven, did word come to us that Cain, our foreparents' first born, had been killed. His house, which he had built, fell upon him and he died in the midst of the house, and was killed by its stones. For by a stone he had slain his brother Abel, and by a stone was he killed in righteous judgment.

As time passed men continued to reproduce, multiply, and fill the earth. The earth was full of wickedness. My prophecies concerning the offspring of the Evil Watchers were long since coming to pass. The earth was saturated in devilry. The decades came, and the decades passed with no visitation from the Lord. Our only reminders of the Lord were the cherubim with the flaming sword, the ever-present never-sleeping guardians of the Paradise gate.

Two hundred and seventy-eight years had elapsed since my calling by Jah-el to pronounce His reprimand upon the

Evil Watchers. Fifty-seven years gone by since the death of Adam. I was now three hundred sixty-five years of age, my son Methuselah three hundred and his son Lamech one hundred and thirteen.

It was in this most glorious year of my life that once again was I visited by the lights of heaven, by they who are the angels Gabriel and Uriel. It was at twilight, warm and clear, when my son and I had adjourned from our labor in our fields, when to our amazement the messengers of God appeared not more than fifteen feet from our abode. Methuselah fell prostrate to the ground, his face etched in sudden horror. Then the angel Gabriel touched him tenderly and said, "Fear not." Gabriel looked deeply into my eyes, communicating a warmth that seemed like friendship. I was ecstatic as I heard him say, "Enoch, the Lord Jah-el summons you." Without preparation was I borne aloft, my son Methuselah gawking upward spellbound by his father's ascension. As I watched him disappear into the oblivion created by great distance, I was weeping tears of joy. Gabriel had said that He would call me again, and now had come that time! I had some further purpose in His plan, but what? Through the cosmos we streaked until we came again to that familiar structure, angels everywhere. The beauty of God's palace far excelled even my most vivid memory. I would forsake all to live in His presence. I cannot describe the joy that is the Lord Jah-el.

Once again was I set before His presence. Once again was I bathed in the heavenly ointment, and appareled in the vesture that transformed me as one of the holy ones. Then the Lord of hosts greeted me saying, "Thou faithful and righteous man Enoch. Blessed are you that you fear Me, and observe My commandments. Blessed are you amongst men that you are called according to My special purpose." Upon hearing the magnificence and majesty of the Lord I kneeled before Him, arms spread forward on the throne platform. I said, "Blessed are You Lord, for You are the giver of all life. Blessed am I, a lowly man, to have found favor in Your eyes." With that the angels of heaven broke forth in loud applause, shouting in one accord, "Blessed is the Lord Jah-el, for He is master of man's destiny. Blessed is the man Enoch for he is chosen of Jah-el."

Then the Lord summoned one of the angels whose name is Pravuel. He is one of the angels that keep the heavenly books. He is quicker in knowledge and wisdom than any of the others in his station who write all the deeds of the Lord. Jah-el spoke to Pravuel and said, "Bring out the books from My storehouses and a reed of quick writing and give it to Enoch, and deliver to him the choice and comforting books." As they were delivered I began to write of all the works of heaven, earth, and sea, and all of the elements, their passages and goings, and the goings and changing of stars, the seasons, years, days, and hours, the risings of the wind, the number of the angels and the formation of their songs, and all human things, the commandments and instructions of Jah-el to usward, and all things that were fitting to learn. After writing all these things then Pravuel said to me, "Enoch, all the things that I have told you you have written. Now sit and write all the souls of mankind, however many of them that are born, and the places prepared for them unto eternity; for all souls are prepared unto eternity from before the setting of the foundation of the world."

For the space of sixty days did I write both day and night, but was not fatigued in any fashion. When my writing came to completion had I a compilation of three hundred and sixty-six books. Then the Lord Jah-el summoned the angel Raphael, dismissing Pravuel for his task was complete. And the Lord said, "Raphael, make known to the man Enoch the holding places of the spirits of men at their death." Then the angel flew over to me and placed both his hands upon my eyes, and lo was I enraptured in a vision.

In the vision the angel took me to a place where stood a great and high mountain of hard rock. And there was carved inside the mountain three hollow places, deep and wide and very smooth. How smooth and dark were two of the hollow places, but one was as the sun with a river of liquid light flowing through it. In complete bewilderment I asked the angel the meaning of these places. Raphael answered, "These hollow places have been created for this purpose, that the spirits of the souls of the dead should assemble therein; yea, that all the souls of the children of men assemble here. These places have been made to receive them till the day of their judgment, and till the appointed period, till the great judgment comes upon them." In these places I saw the spirits of the children of men who were dead, and their voices cried out to heaven. Then I perceived a spirit in the lighted hollow who was persistent in his complaint, and I asked Raphael, "Who is this soul?" He answered saying, "This is the spirit which came forth from Abel, whom Cain slew, and he makes suit against him till his seed is destroyed from off the face of the earth, and his seed annihilated from amongst the seed of men." Then I asked regarding the hollow places, as to why each was separated from the other. Raphael answered and said unto me, "These three have been made that the spirits of the dead should be separated. And such a division has been made for the spirits of the righteous, in which there is the bright river of water. The second division is for those sinners who lived prosperously, having escaped punishment in life. The third division is for the sinners who suffer in their lives and therefore incur a lesser penalty in Sheol, but their finality is the same as those in the second division." At that moment I recalled my first journey to heaven and the terrible place shown to me, the place prepared for the satans, the place of eternal fire and gloom, that place with the cruel instruments of torture. The eternal resting place of all who find disfavor in the eyes of the Lord Jah-el. Raphael continued, "These in this division are the suffering unrighteous who cry out to the Lord for vengeance upon those who occupy the second division. But He hears them not. They cry out in vain, for He hears only the voices of the righteous from this place." When I awoke from the vision Raphael's hands were removed from my eyes. He was sent back to his place, his Master's bidding complete. I pondered, sitting as though carved of stone myself. Then the Lord spoke to me saying, "Do you understand Enoch?" I answered Him in affirmation.

After some space of silence, Jah-el allowing me time to assimilate all that I had seen motioned me to an intimate audience. He said,

"Enoch, beloved, all that thou seest, all things that are standing finished, all this I created from non being; the visible things from invisible. Hear Enoch, and take in these My words, for not to My angels have I told my secret, nor My endless realm, nor have they understood My creating, which I tell thee today. For before all things were visible I alone used to go about in the invisible things, like the sun from east to west and west to east. But even the sun has peace in itself but at that time I found none because I was creating all things, and I conceived the thought of placing foundations and of creating visible creation. And I did so in six days, and this seventh is My day of rest. And I had in mind to appoint the eighth day also, that the eighth day should be the first created after My work, and that the first seven revolve in the form of seven thousand, and at the beginning of the eight thousand there should be a time of not counting; endless, with neither years, nor months, nor weeks, nor days, nor hours. But alas, your father Adam fell from perfection. Have no fear Enoch, for all things shall be as I have purposed from the beginning. Through you Enoch, shall the beginning of the redemption plan of Jah-el be made known to mankind. And now, Enoch, all that I have told thee, all that thou hast understood, and all that thou hast seen of heavenly things, all that thou hast seen on earth, and all that I have written in books by my great wisdom, all these things I have devised and created from the uppermost foundation to the lower and to the end, and there is no counselor nor inheritor to my creations. I am self-eternal, not made with hands, and without change. My thought is My counselor. My wisdom and My word are My determination, and My eyes observe all things how they stand and tremble with terror in My presence. If I turn away My face then all things are destroyed.

Now apply thy mind Enoch, and know Him who is speaking to thee, and take thou the books that thou hast written. Now I give thee Gabriel and Uriel who led thee up, and the books, and go back down to the earth and tell thy sons all that I have made known to thee, and all that thou hast seen, from the lower heavens up to My throne, and all the troops. For I created all forces, and there is none that resisteth me or that does not subject himself to me. For all subject themselves to my monarchy and labor for my sole rule.

Give them the books of thy handwriting and they

will read them, and know Me for the Creator of all things, and will understand how there is no other God but Me. And let them distribute the books of thy handwriting, children to children, generation to generation, nations to nations."

The Lord of Glory stopped short his sayings to me. He reared back upon His throne of power, bringing the almighty forefinger of His right hand to His lips. He paused in contemplative thought for some seconds, then continued,

"Enoch my intercessor, say this to the wicked and perverse of men. Tell them that God convicts the idolaters and the sodomite fornicators, and therefore brings down a deluge upon them. They have rejected My commandments and My yoke. Worthless seeds have come up, not fearing Me. They will not bow to Me, but bow to vain gods. They have denied My union and have laden the whole earth with lies, offences, abominable lecheries, namely one with another, and all manner of unclean wickedness, which are disgusting to My sight. Therefore will I bring a deluge upon the entire earth, and will destroy all men, and the whole earth will crumble into great darkness. But Enoch, one shall proceed from your seed. In him shall I please Myself according to My will, and because of him shall his family be redeemed. And behold, after the destruction, from their seed shall arise another generation much afterwards. But of them many will be insatiate. He that shall be of your seed shall raise that generation to My consciousness, and reveal to them the books of your writing. To the faithful men, and workers of my pleasure shall he tell them of Me. And they shall tell another generation, and those others having read shall be glorified thereafter more than the first."

Then the Lord Jah-el commanded that I should go back to earth for the space of thirty days, to relay these His instructions. After thirty days was I to return, and remain until the Lord's future use. These are the exact words of the Lord Jah-el on my behalf, "Now Enoch I give you the term of thirty days to spend in thy house, and tell thy sons and all thy household that all may hear from My mouth what is told them by thee. That they may read and understand, how there is no other God but Me. And after thirty days shall my angels take thee from earth. They shall take thee from thy wife and thy sons. For you shall not taste of death in your appropriate time, but in a time far and distant."

After these sayings the Lord Jah-el summoned forth one of the seraphim, terrible and menacing, and placed him by me. He was in appearance as alabaster, and his hands like polished crystals. He touched my face and my face became as his, hardened and polished like the crystal of the throne platform floor did my face become, that I might endure the presence of the Lord. For sitting in the presence of the Lord Jah-el is as a man sitting in the presence of the sun. Then the Lord said to me, "Enoch, if thy face were not touched no man on earth would be able to behold thy face." The Lord Jah-el then called forth Gabriel and Uriel, and said to them, "Let Enoch go down to earth with you, and I give you permission to await him till the determined day of his translation."

It was in the deep of night that I was returned, to the very spot from whence I was taken. My son Methuselah, anticipating my return, had camped at the spot of my ascension, keeping watch day and night. He was filled with great awe at the sound of my coming and upon my feet touching the ground, I embraced him in the love that a father has for his son. While in the presence of Jah-el His words of my return had not affected me adversely, but in the absence of His glory my heart became sore distressed. At the end of these thirty days I would never feel the warmth of my beloved Edni again, nor ever till the soil alongside my strong Methuselah. I would become an alien resident in the kingdom of Jah-el, with no other human for companionship.

My son was as if transferred back to the days of his childhood, an endless stream of questions gushing from his lips. I said to him, "Methuselah, go on ahead, wake everyone in our settlement, that I may tell all everything." For twenty-nine days did the people sit before me as I gave them my writings, and the explanations there of. They sat in great awe and amazement, soaking up my words as the flora did the morning mist. It was now the thirtieth day, a day of sorrow for my family, a day of sorrow for me. I had attempted to devote as much time as I could to Edni, but the clamor for more information was so great from the people. While I know that her heart was breaking she portrayed that strength that was one of the attributes I loved her for so dearly. If it was death that was taking me, she confided, she would be better equipped to handle the loss. But to look into the heavens each and every day of her life, knowing that I was alive seemed a cruelty. In this low estate of earth I shared Edni's conclusion, "But," I said, "He is God." "Yes," she said, "He is."

On the final day, the children quaked in their mothers' arms as I relayed to them the vision of the hollow places. I recalled to them from my first heavenly visit how I had seen the key holders, and the guardians of the gates of hell, standing like great serpents, and their faces like extinguished lamps, and their eyes of fire, and their sharp teeth. "This," I said, "is the destiny of all who fall into the second and third holding place of spirits."

As the time of my departure grew closer, a sense of urgency for the welfare of those I would leave behind overwhelmed me. I spoke to them ever so pointedly saying,

"As one year is more honorable than another so is one man more honorable than another—some for great possessions, some for wisdom of heart, some for particular intellect, some for cunning; one for longsuffering, another for cleanliness, one for strength, another for comeliness; one for youth, another for sharp wit, one for shape of body, another for sensibility. Let it be heard everywhere, there is none better than he who fears God for he shall be more glorious in times to come. And now my people, lay thought on your hearts, mark well my words, which have come to you from the Lord's lips. Take these books and read them, for the books are many. In them will you learn all the works and all that has been from the beginning of creation, and will be to the end of time. If you will observe these writings, you will not sin against the Lord for there is no other except Him. He has placed the foundation of the universe in the unknown, and has spread forth heavens visible and invisible. He fixed the earth on the water, and created countless creatures. Who has counted the drops of water that fill the sea, or the dust of the earth, or the sands of the seashore? He cut the stars out of His fire and decorated the heavens.

In my absence my people do not say that I am standing before God praying for your sins, for there I am not your helper. Pray to the Lord Jah-el, for He is merciful to the humble in spirit. So my people mark well all the words that I am giving you, lest you regret saying why did Enoch not tell us? Let these books be an inheritance of your peace. Hand them to all who want them, and instruct them, that they may see the Lord's great and many marvelous works.

My people behold, the day of my term and time has approached. The angels who shall bear me are standing before me, and urge me to my departure. Therefore I bid you do before the Lord's face all His good pleasure."

My son slowly stood, tears streaming down his cheeks, "Father," he cried, "What is agreeable to your eyes, that I may make before your face, that you may bless our dwellings, and your sons, and that the people may be made glorious through you, and then may you depart as the Lord Jah-el has decreed." I answered, "Hear my words my son, and be not dismayed by them. I wish nothing. For from the time when the Lord anointed me with the ointment of His glory, there has been no food in me. My soul remembers not earthly enjoyment. Neither do I crave anything earthly, but I shall give you my blessing."

I gathered Edni, Methuselah, his brethren Regim, Riman, Uchan, Chermion, Gaidad, and all the elders, and all the people, and I blessed them, and said to them the instructions of Jah-el. Then the people began to fall upon my neck, and to kiss me, and to say, "Enoch, be thou blessed of the Lord the eternal ruler. For you shall be glorified before the Lord's face at all times. For the Lord chose you from amongst all men, and designated you a scribe of all His creation visible and invisible." Then I answered the people, saying,

"Hear my people, before all creatures were

created the Lord created the visible and invisible things. Then He created man in His own likeness and form. He put into us eyes to see, and ears to hear, a heart to reflect, and an intellect to deliberate. Then He divided time and from time He fixed years, and from years He appointed months, and from months, days, and of days He appointed seven in the likeness of His own. In the days He appointed hours, measured out exactly, that man might reflect on time and count years, months, hours, their alternation, beginning, and end, and that he might count his own life, from the beginning until death.

When all creation visible and invisible shall end, and every man goes to the great judgment, afterwards shall all counting of time cease. The crack in infinity shall be healed. There will be one eon, and all the righteous who will escape the Lord's great judgment shall be collected therein. For the righteous shall this great eon begin, and they shall live eternally. They shall not suffer labor, nor sickness, nor humiliation, nor anxiety, nor need, nor violence, nor night, nor darkness, but great light. They shall have a great indestructible wall, and a paradise bright, and shall put on incorruptible, for all corruptible things shall pass away, and life will be everlasting. My people, keep your souls from all injustice such as the Lord hates."

When I had finished these words did the Lord send out darkness upon the face of the earth, and it covered all those standing and talking with me. Then the angels Gabriel and Uriel lifted me, and they took me again to the highest heaven where the Lord Jah-el dwells. After my translation did the darkness leave the earth, for it was only to cloak my departure. And the people neither saw nor understood how I had been taken. Then did my son Methuselah and his brethren make haste, and erected an altar at the place called Achuzan—the place of my translation. They sacrificed oxen to the Lord Jah-el and they made a great feast, rejoicing, and making merry three days, praising God that He had given them a sign in me. A sign, and books, to pass on to generation after generation, to let them know that the righteous shall see the face of the Lord and live forever world without end.

I was born on the sixth day of the month Tsivan, and I lived three hundred and sixty-five years on the surface of the earth. I walked, and talked with the Lord Jah-el. I was then I was not, for the Lord Jah-el took me.

CHAPTER 8

NOAH

In the one hundred thirteenth year of my grandson Lamech's life, had the Lord Jah-el taken me. Lamech had taken to wife Betenos, the daughter of Barakiil, the daughter of his father's brother. When Lamech was one hundred eighty-two years of age, she bore him a son and they called him Noah. It is he that Jah-el had spoken of as the continuance of mankind.

Sixty-nine years had elapsed since my translation. My son Methuselah was now three hundred sixty-nine. Our aged father Adam was now dead one hundred twenty-six years. It was my assignment whilst I was in heaven to view the activities of men. It was the will of the Lord Jah-el that I write in volumes the unfolding of His divine plan. As I was called, so He was calling others. He revealed to me all. I witnessed all down through the corridor of time. I've seen the beginning, the middle, and the end. It is why I am the teller of His story.

The dark lord Lucifer, he that was now called Satan, was idle in his activity. There was no need for him to bother the earth, for his fallen angels and their wicked offspring were filling the coffers of Sheol. The second and third divisions of the holding place of the spirits of men were being added to at a ravenous pace. The dark lord Lucifer was now master of the earth, but what a miniscule victory in light of what was in store for him at the end of the age. He knew he was defeated. He knew his demise was at the Lord Jah-el's whim. What he did not know was how. But no matter, for the dark lord had decreed that in his fate he would not be alone. He would take as many souls of mankind with him as he possibly could, and judging the celerity of increase of the souls of men into his portion of Sheol there would be the majority. He and his angelic cronies would bring unfathomable horrors to these souls for eternity. They would forever pay the price of their fury.

The next five hundred years of human history proved to be the most decadent in the eyesight of the Lord Jah-el. All of heaven sensed His divine displeasure. In the meanwhile had the man Noah grew in stature and grace. He had taken to wife Emzara, the daughter of Rakeel his father's brother, and by the time Noah was five hundred years of age, she had bore him three sons: Shem, Ham, and Japheth. They too had come of age, and had taken wives of their own.

My son Methuselah was now eight hundred sixty-nine years old, and Lamech six hundred eighty-two. Adam was now six hundred twenty-six years dead, and would have been one thousand five hundred fifty-six had he not sinned. It was five hundred sixty-nine years since my translation. Enos had died eighty-four years into the life of Noah, Cainan one hundred seventy-nine years into his life, Mahalalel two hundred thirty-four years into his life, and my father Jared three hundred sixty-six years into the life of Noah. These faithful men, along with countless others, had succumbed to death and their spirits deposited in the holding place of the righteous.

The Lord Jah-el looked down from on high, and viewed the wickedness of man. It was great in the earth and their every thought, their every imagination, was evil continuously. And it pained the Lord that He had made man; it grieved Him to his heart. Then the Lord decreed, "I will destroy man, whom I have created, from off the face of the earth. I will destroy the beasts, the creeping things, and the fowls of the air, for it pains Me that I made them."

But Noah found favor in the eyes of Jah-el, and in the four hundred eightieth year of Noah's life did the Lord speak to him, saying,

"Noah, the end of all flesh is come before Me for the earth is filled with violence, and behold I will destroy them. It is My decree that you should build an ark, for I shall destroy the world by water. I shall cause a new thing, a wonder, for I shall cause it to rain. Therefore, build the ark according to My instruction. Make it of gopher wood. Rooms shall you make in it, and you shall tar it within and without. Make the length of it four hundred and fifty feet, the breadth of it seventy-five feet, and the height forty-five feet. A window shall thou make in this ark, eighteen inches high, around the entire top of the ark. You shall also set in the side of this ark a door, and the ark shall be of three levels. For behold I shall bring a flood of water upon all the earth, and every thing that is on the earth shall die. But with thee Noah shall I establish a covenant and thou shall come out of this ark, thou, and thy sons, and thy wife, and thy sons' wives with thee.

Of all animals bring two into the ark; one male, one female, and of the cattle of the earth two. Of every creeping thing two, that they may be preserved alive. And take thou into the ark all food that is eaten of yourselves and the animals, and thou shalt gather it together and store it as food."

Noah did as the Lord Jah-el commanded, he and his house. For the space of one hundred and twenty years did Noah and his family construct the ark. For one hundred and twenty years did Noah preach the coming destruction, suffering ridicule from both neighbor and friend alike for never had water fallen from the sky. How sad it was for me to view this scene from heaven, for I had seen with my own eyes the vast storehouse of water suspended around the globe. The people of earth lambasted Noah for the building of the monstrosity that he called the ark. They howled with laughter and of them all only Lamech, and my aged son Methuselah believed.

One hundred and twenty years later did the Lord once more speak to Noah. Noah was now six hundred years old. Lamech, Noah's father, whose life Seth had died one hundred sixty years into was now dead himself. He had passed on as Seth to the hollow place of the faithful. Lamech died five years prior to the falling of the flood waters, five hundred ninety-five years into Noah's life did he die. I had now been translated for six hundred sixty-nine years. Adam was now seven hundred twenty-six years gone, and would have seen one thousand six hundred fifty-six years had he not sinned, and my aged son Methuselah was now nine hundred sixty-nine. These are the ages of all those who did pass before me. Adam was nine hundred thirty years at his death, Seth nine hundred twelve, Enos nine hundred five, Cainan nine hundred ten, Mahalalel eight hundred ninety-five, Jared nine hundred sixty-two, Lamech seven hundred seventy-seven, but my son Methuselah lived longer than any man on the face of the earth, and did die in the same year of the falling of the waters from heaven.

The Lord Jah-el spoke to Noah, and said, "Noah come thou and all thy house into the ark, and bring in with thee seven of every clean beast and seven of the fowl of the air. Bring into the ark all that you have prepared for in seven days shall I cause it to rain, and it shall pour forty days and forty nights." Noah did according to the Lord's command and the people came up from their dens of corruption, their cities, to make mockery of Noah. For seven days did Noah and his family make final preparation of the ark, and in those seven days did the crowds become louder. They brought food, and drink to toast this idiotic occasion. "Beware," they shouted to one another, reeling in their revelry, "it's going to rain." Noah and his family continued their labor, turning deaf ears to the crowd. Noah knew that if the Lord Jah-el said in seven days He would do this thing, in seven days it would be done.

It came to be the seventh day, and the voice of the Lord came to Noah saying, "The time is at hand." The multitude without the ark gasped in amazement as the door of the ark was fitted into place without hands. The Lord Jah-el gave the decree, and the seven angels that held the seven floodgates of the waters that were suspended above the earth were commanded to release them. At first the people could not believe their eyes, as they saw pellets of falling water colliding into the earth. Fear gripped their bowels as a drowning man grips flotsam, and how soon would this analogy become their reality. It was raining; water was actually falling from the sky. Then the people believed and made frantic haste toward the ark. They screamed and pleaded for Noah to open the door. He could not, for God had sealed the door knowing that Noah was a man of great compassion. They could view from the upper portals the chaotic state of their fellow men. The angels of Jah-el thwarted any attempts of the wicked to board the ark. Those on the outside hysterically clawed with their hands at the door of the ark until their fingernails were left embedded in the wood, and their fingertips reduced to bloody stumps. Everywhere was terror! Noah and his family wept tears of pity as the days passed. They heard the relentlessness of the pouring rain, and the ever decreasing sounds of desperation from outside the ark—until there was nothing but complete and eerie silence.

It rained as the Lord had said, forty days and forty nights, until the floodgates of heaven were emptied. The earth was now as it was in the beginning, globally immersed in water. Twenty two feet above the highest mountain did the water cover the earth, and for a total of one hundred fifty days did the waters remain at that level so that all flesh was erased. One thousand six hundred fifty-six years of man's history had passed, and now was the dawning of a new genesis.

CHAPTER 9

THE AFTERMATH

On the two hundred twenty-fourth day after the onset of the rain had the waters receded sufficient for the ark to rest upon the mountains of Ararat. Seemingly magical occurrences were birthed to the earth due to the flood. For the first time in history was man able to view the sun and the moon in total clarity. Even the color of the sky had changed. In daylight it was no longer a muted bluish green, but was now breathtakingly blue. Now there were clouds, fluffy, white, and massive. Noah and his family were initially greatly disturbed by the added brightness, but equally compensated by the novel spectacles they viewed. At night the heavens had become an ink black backdrop, contrasting in high resolution the breath taking paths of shooting stars. The stars were now so amazingly clear, and never had they realized them to be so numerous. Phenomena of second heaven once seen only by my own eyes, after the falling of the waters were now more clearly visible to these eight surviving souls. Another occurrence that greatly concerned Noah was the cold. Something was different about the air. It was no longer tropical. They had no way of realizing that the poles of the earth were freezing, for when the earth was encapsulated it held the sun's warmth. Now that the insulating water blanket was gone, through process of evaporation, and condensation, rain, snow, and ice would now become natural to planet Earth.

The earth had soaked in a great deal of the water, while evaporation took its due to the heavens'. Three hundred and seventy-one days after Noah entered the ark did he step upon dry ground. He and his family were repulsed by what assaulted their vision. The earth was damp and hostile. Nothing moved; everything was drowned. The earth was a sickening gray; decayed remains littered the countryside. Globally the habitable land was reduced by the additional water upon the earth. There were new oceans, seas, lakes, mountains, and valleys. The weight of the water had made the earth's crust less stable and subject to increased seismic activity. The earth and all therein was exhausted.

The Lord Jah-el once again spoke to Noah, and instructed him to release all of the animals brought into the ark. Afterwards Noah built an altar and sacrificed an array of clean animals, as well as incense of odor to the Lord. The Lord Jah-el was pleased with Noah's offering and spoke to him, making a covenant with him, promising that never again would He destroy the earth with water, and as a sign of that covenant He placed the rainbow in the sky. Jah-el blessed Noah and his family, reiterating the procreation mandate. He told Noah that now all animal life was given to mankind as food and clothing but man was never to eat the blood thereof, for blood was sacred because it is the life and all life belongs to Jah-el. The Lord Jah-el also warned Noah that because of this decree would the animals of the earth grow to fear man, for now man was divinely mandated a hunter. Noah and his sons acknowledged the law of Jah-el, and all swore that they would not consume the blood.

In the six hundred and first year of his life did Noah set foot on the land, and in that year did he and his sons clear a place for themselves and they began to plant their seed stock. And Noah planted vines on the mountain and for a full three years did he guard the vines. And so it came to pass that at the very onset of the fourth year that he gathered the fruit thereof and made for himself wine which he aged for an additional year's time. At the fifth year anniversary of their coming forth from the ark Noah presided over what had now become an annual family celebration of offering sacrifices to the Lord, and rejoicing and praising Him that He had saved them. Afterwards Noah brought forth his fermentation of the vine and did drink himself into inebriation, he and his household with him. At the close of the day, the festivities well ended, Noah retired to his tent. Being drunk, he disrobed and fell asleep naked upon his bed. Ham discovered his father's condition, and proceeded to make sport of it to his brethren. But Shem and Japheth were not amused; and so walking backwards, so as not to see their father's shame, covered him with a cloak. When Noah awakened and was told of his son's folly he became sore enraged, and cursed Ham's infant son Canaan saying, "Cursed be Canaan, an enslaved servant shall he be to his brethren." Thus Noah cursed Ham's baby son, knowing that this would afflict Ham even more than had the curse been made upon him. Then Noah continued, "Blessed be the Lord God of Shem, and Canaan shall be his servant. God shall enlarge Japheth, and cause him to prosper."

Upon hearing of the curse leveled against his youngest son, Ham was incensed. Then he, his wife, and his sons Cush, Mizraim, Put, and Canaan departed from his father, and Ham built his own settlement and called it

Ne'elatama'uk. Japheth saw what his brother had done and became envious of him, and so he and his family left Noah and built a settlement and called it Adataneses. Shem eventually followed suit and built his family's camp close to those of his father and brethren on the mountain, and called its name Sedeqetelebab. These are the sons of Shem shortly after his disembarking the ark: Elam, Asshur, Arpachshad, Lud, and Arram. And the sons of Japheth: Gomer, Magog, Madai, Juvan, Tubal, Meshech, and Tiras.

In the course of time many more sons and daughters were born to the sons of Noah, and these intermarried. Arpachshad, Shem's son born in the second year after the flood, grew to manhood and took to wife Rasu'eja, the daughter of Susan, the daughter of Elam, who was also Shem's son. Rasu'eja bore a son and his name was called Kainam, and when he grew his father taught him writing. When he became of age he set out to find a suitable place of settlement that he might marry and father his children. In the midst of his quest did he come upon a writing that was carved on a rock. He transcribed it and sinned owing to it for it contained the teachings of the Evil Watchers in accordance with which they used to observe the omens of the sun, moon, and stars. So he wrote out the sayings and said nothing to Noah concerning it, fearing that Noah would be angered. So Kainam found his place and took to wife Melka the daughter of Madai, the son of Japheth. Then Melka bore a son to Kainam, and they named him Shelah. Shelah came of age, and took to wife Mu'ak. Mu'ak bore him a son, and he was named Eber. Eber grew, and took to wife Azurad. She bore him a son, and they called his name Peleg. In the days of Peleg did the sons of Noah begin to divide the earth. They divided in three parts, in lots. Shem's lot became the middle of the earth, which was to become his and the inheritance of his children. So Shem's land extended from the middle of the Ural Mountains; from the mouth of the water from the river Tanais westward to where this same river empties into the sea of Azov. All lands to the north are Japheth's, but all land to the south down to the reaches of the Egyptian border was allotted to Shem. His portion extended west in a straight line to the Egyptian Sea, south to Africa to the extent of the Nile, and east toward Eden.

To Ham was allotted the second portion, beyond the Gi'hon, towards the south to the right of Eden, to the mountains of fire, and it extended to the west to the newly formed Atlantic Ocean, and even farther west to Oceanus. To the north as far as Cadiz, and it goes forth to the coast of the waters of the sea to the waters of the Great Sea till it draws near to the river Gi'hon, and runs along the Gi'hon until it reaches the right of Eden.

To Japheth was allotted the final portion beyond the river Tanais, northeast to the whole region of Scythia, and to all land east there-of. It extends northerly to the mountains of Celt, toward Oceanus, and it goes forth to the east of Cadiz as far as the sea. It extends until it approaches the west of Fara, and it returns toward Aferag, and it extends easterly to the sea of Azov. It extends to the region of the Tanais River in a northeasterly direction until it approaches the boundary of its waters toward the Ural Mountains, and it turns round to the north. So Japheth received five great islands, and a great land in the north, in a land that is cold. Ham's land is intense in heat, and the land of Shem is neither hot nor cold but is blended of both.

Ham then divided his land amongst his sons and the first portion did he give to Cush the lands toward the east, and to the west of him for Mizraim, and to the west of him for Put. Shem also divided amongst his sons; the first portion went to Elam to the east of the river Tigris till it approaches all of the land of India. To Asshur came the second portion, all the land of Asshur, and Nineveh, and Shinar, and to the borders of India. To Arpachshad all the land of the region of the Chaldees to the east of the Euphrates bordering on the Red sea, and all the land of Lebanon, Sanir, and Amana to the border of the Euphrates. To Aram, all the land of Mesopotamia between the Tigris and the Euphrates toward the north of the Chaldees to the border of the land of Asshur and the land of Arara. To Lud the mountains of Asshur and all therein till it reaches the Great Sea, and till it reaches the east of Asshur his brother. Japheth also divided his land so that in the far-reaching future his son Magog would become father of the Russian people, and Meshech and Tubal the fathers of the Turks, Madai the father of the Britons, Tiras the father of the Thracians, and Javan the father of the Greeks. From Cush would stem the Ethiopians; from Mizraim, the Egyptians; from Elam, the Orientals; from Put, the Libyans. The allotting of the land was in the permissive will of the Lord Jahel, for it was in the distinctions of these peoples that He would play out His master plan.

At the onset of the falling of the floodwaters had the Lord Jah-el dispatched Michael and a legion of His holy angels. He sent them to dematerialize the two hundred Evil Watchers and to cast them into their holding places until the final judgment. These would not lead astray mankind ever again except for the five that were bound in the earth for a tribulation time far into the future. With these restrained, the dark lord Lucifer was forced from his relative ease of not having to coerce mankind into wickedness. As Jah-el had decreed hundreds of years afore this time, the earth was now being roamed by the disembodied spirits of the Nephilim, Eljo, and Eluid. Those neither human nor angelic beings who were now the invisible monstrosities of that unholy union. There was no place found for them in heaven, and no place for them in Sheol, and being in between worlds they strove to occupy bodies anew, for from bodies were they cast forth. It was by these wicked demon spirits that the dark lord Lucifer would wreak new havoc upon this new generation of mankind. He already had Kainam's whetted appetite for the mysteries of the dark passages. Envy had already raised its ugly head amongst brothers, and now had the sons of Noah secretly divided the known earth that they may have individual possession instead of living as one family of man. Satan could see the pervasiveness of his evil far into the future. With his fallen angels, and the wicked demon spirits, he would lure countless captives into his partitions of the underworld.

So the dark lord Lucifer left his domain and called all the evil spirits to himself, and they bowed before his presence and did obeisance before him. Satan commanded them saying, "Plague the children of the earth and seek to inhabit and destroy their souls, that I may use them as pawns to unrighteousness and to cause sorrow to Jah-el through His worthless creatures of flesh and blood. Go forth and do as I have commanded." There was no real sense of purpose in these disembodied spirits prior to Satan's edict, but now they had a leader and their leader became their power. The spirits went forth attempting to possess whom they could, to work out once more the evil desires that consumed them. Without bodies they cannot experience the sensations of their wicked lust but with them would they reintroduce into the world antediluvian mass murders, serial killings, witchcraft, sorceries, idolatry, adulteries, gross fornication, sodomy, and all practices sore displeasing to the Lord of hosts.

The unclean spirits began to lead astray the children of

the sons of Noah and to make them err from my writings, and to destroy them. Noah's sons approached him and relayed to him the activities of the demons. Noah cried out to the Lord Jah-el, praying, "God of the spirits of all flesh who has shown mercy towards me, You who saved us from the waters of the flood, and have not caused me to perish as you did the sons of perdition, and have allowed us to live, and multiply in increase. Lord Thou knowest how the Evil Watchers, the fathers of these evil spirits, acted in my day, and for these spirits which are living I pray Thee imprison them, and let them not bring destruction upon my offspring." But Satan was in heaven, expecting Noah's plea, and he bade audience before Jah-el. "Lord Creator," he petitioned, "Please allow some of them to remain before me that they may listen to my voice and do my bidding. For these are for leading astray, for the sons of men are wicked." Then the Lord decreed that all but a tenth of them should be bound, and the remaining did the angels of heaven bind in the place of eternal condemnation.

The Lord Jah-el sent words to Noah of all of the ways of the malignant spirits, that his sons might recognize their wiles, and Noah wrote these in a book and gave it to his beloved son Shem. Shortly after this occurrence did Noah die, and he was buried on Mount Lubar in the land of Ararat. Noah's life spanned nine hundred fifty years, then his spirit was transported to the place of the called. Three hundred forty-nine years had now elapsed from the time of Noah's setting foot from the ark. Two thousand six years had elapsed from Adam's creation to Noah's death, and I had been in heaven one thousand nineteen years.

These are the generations of the sons of Noah—Shem, Ham, and Japheth: unto them were sons born after the flood. The sons of Japheth were Gomer, Magog, Madai, Javan,

Tubal, Meshech, and Tiras. The sons of Gomer were
Ashkenaz, Riphath, and Togarmah. The sons of Javan were
Elishah, Tarshish, Kittim, and Dodanim.

And the sons of Ham were Cush, Mizraim, Put, and
Canaan. The sons of Cush were Seba, Havilah, Sabtah,
Raamah, and Sabtecha. Of the sons of Raamah were Sheba
and Dedan. Cush begat Nimrod—who began to be a mighty
one in the earth; the beginning of his kingdom was Babel—
and Erech, Accad, and Calneh, in the land of Shinar, and the
cities Rehoboth, Calah, and Resen. Mizraim begat Ludim,
Anamim, Lehabim, Naphtuhim, Pathrusim, and Casluhim
out of whom came Philistim and Caphtorim. Canaan begat
Sidon his firstborn, and Heth. From Canaan's lineage eventually sprang the Jebusite, the Amorite, the Girgasite, the
Hivite, the Arkite, the Sinite, the Arvadite, the Zemarite,
and the Hamathite, and afterward were the families of these
Canaanites spread abroad in great number in a land not their
own, but that of Shem's.

And the children of Shem were Elam, and Asshur who
built Nineveh, and Arpachshad, Lud, and Aram. The children of Aram were Uz, Hul, Gether, and Mash. Arpachshad
begat Salah; and Salah begat Eber. Unto Eber were born two
sons: Peleg; for in his days was the earth divided; and his
brother Joktan. Joktan begat Almodad, Sheleph, Hazar-
maveth, Jerah, Hadoram, Uzal, Diklah, Obal, Abimael,
Sheba, Ophir, Havilah, and Jobab. These are the families of
the sons of Noah, after their generations, in their nations:
and by these were the nations established in the earth after
the flood.

CHAPTER 10

ABRAHAM AND ISAAC

P eleg the son of Eber, who was of the line of Shem, took
to wife Lomna. She bore him a son and he called his
name Reu, which means *evil*, for Peleg was marking by his
son's name his impression of the times. It was in the days of
Peleg that men choose to forsake a portion of the procreative mandate of the Lord Jah-el given Noah and his sons.
Instead of spreading out anew toward repopulation of the
land they, under Nimrod's leadership, decided to congregate
in one place for the purpose of building for themselves a
great city and strong tower. It was said that this tower would
be built as an escape if the Lord Jah-el should destroy the
earth by water a second time. They built upon this tower for
forty-three laborious years. Then the Lord Jah-el grew
wearisome of their vanity, and said within Himself, "Let Us
go down to the surface of the earth and confound the
language of the people, for they are all of one tongue." Then
the Lord touched the mouths of all the people of the earth
and they began to speak in divers tongues. Confusion
abounded and the people abruptly ceased their building.
Then Jah-el sent a mighty wind and overthrew the tower,

and the people scattered over the entire earth each in the company of those who spoke their new language. And the place of the tower in each new tongue became known by one name: *Babel.*

Ham and his sons proceeded to go forth and to occupy the land of their allotment but Canaan saw the land of Lebanon to the river of Egypt, that it was very good, and he went not into the land of his inheritance but dwelt in Lebanon. Ham his father, and Cush, and Mizraim his brothers said to him, "Canaan, you have settled in a land that is not yours. Do not dwell in the land of Shem, for to Shem and his sons did this land fall by lot." But he did not hearken, but possessed the land, and for this reason did that region of Shem become known as the land of Canaan. Japheth and his sons moved toward the sea and dwelt in the land of their portion, but Madai spied out the land and found it not to his liking. He in turn begged a portion of land from Elam, Asshur, and Arpachshad, and his dwelling place came to be known as Media, and eventually into the far distant future as the kingdom of Persia.

Reu the son of Peleg, of the line of Shem, took to himself a wife, and her name was Ora, and she bore him a son, and they called him Serug. In Serug's time did the sons of Noah begin to war with one another, and take captives, and to slay one another, and to spill and drink blood. They built strong cities, walls, and towers, and individuals began to exalt themselves above the nations, and to found kingdoms; all began to practice evil, and acquire arms, and to teach war, and to sell their fellow men into slavery. They made for themselves idols of gold, wood, and clay, and the evil spirits assisted, and seduced them into committing transgression. The dark lord Lucifer exerted himself to do all this, and he sent forth his angelic brethren to corrupt and destroy. Serug grew up and dwelt in Shinar, in the land of the Chaldees. He took to himself a wife, and her name was Melka, and she bore him Nahor his son. As Nahor grew, Serug taught him the ways of the Chaldees—divining and augury—and astrology.

Nahor took to himself a wife, whose name was I'jaska, and she bore him a son Terah. Terah took a wife, and her name was Edna, and she bore him a son and they called his name Abram. At Abram's birth had I resided in the heaven of Jah-el nine hundred sixty-four years, Adam would have been one thousand nine hundred fifty-one years of age had he not eaten of the forbidden tree. As Abram grew in stature and mind he began to understand the errors of men, how they worshipped idols. At the age of fourteen did young Abram separate himself from the practice of idolatry. Abram began to pray to the Creator of all things that He might save him from the path of the ungodly, and that he should not fall into error. Then it came to pass, that one day Abram approached his father with regard to the futility of bowing before lifeless gods. Terah quickly hushed him, for these gods were his business and brought him great gain. It would not do for the purveyor of idols to openly admit their vanity. It would also not do for the son of an idol maker to express such views openly. Abram obeyed his father, but spoke also of the matter to his brothers. They too rebuked him, and became angry toward him; then Abram spoke of the matter no longer.

Abram took to himself a wife, and her name was Sarai. Haran his brother also took a wife, and she bore him a son and they called his name Lot. The matter of the idols plagued Abram's mind so much so that in the dead of night he set fire to the house of idols, and all that was in the house was burned, and no man knew who had set the fire. But the men arose in the night, attempting to rescue their gods, and Haran hastened to save them and was consumed in the flames. Haran was buried at Ur, of the Chaldees.

Terah, being distraught over the death of his son, packed his belongings and journeyed to the land of Lebanon in Canaan, both he and his entire family, and there remained fourteen years. While there, on a night of the new moon, did Abram sit through the night, observing the stars in regard to the character of rain for the year. While engulfed in the task words came forth from Abram's innermost being, and he prayed, saying, "My God, God most high, You alone are my God. Deliver me from the wiles of the spirits who have dominion over the thoughts of man. Establish me and my seed forever that we may not go astray from henceforth, and evermore." Abram paused for a while, then proceeded to do something that brought great joy and gladness to the Lord Jah-el. Abram began to ask the Lord what should he do with his life, saying, "My God, my Master, what should I do with this life that You have so graciously bestowed to me. What should I do? Where should I go? Shall I return to Ur, or should I remain in this place? Show me my right path O God, and prosper it in the hands of Your servant, that I might fulfill it, and that I may not walk in deceitfulness of heart."

Then the Lord Jah-el spoke to Abram, and said, "Get up from this place Abram, leave thy father's presence, and go unto a land which I shall show you, and I will make you a great nation. I will bless you, and thou shall be a blessing to the earth, and in thee will all families of the earth be blessed. I will be your God, and the God of your son, and the God of your son's son, and the God of all thy seed." Then the Lord Jah-el sent Michael to Abram and designated that Michael become the protecting angel to Abram, and to all Abram's seed until time should cease. Michael, doing

Jah-el's bidding, touched the mouth and ears of Abram that he might hear and speak with the language that had ceased from the earth since Jah-el confused the languages. Then Michael began to speak to Abram in Hebrew, for Hebrew was the language spoken since Jah-el had opened the mouth of Adam that he might converse. Jah-el had discontinued its use from the tower incident, but was now reinstating its usage in the mouth of Abram and his seed. Michael gave Abram the books of my writing for they were written in Hebrew, the tongue of creation. Abram took the books and transcribed them, and began to study them, and Michael made known to Abram all that he did not understand. After the six-month season of the rains did Abram speak of his departure to Terah his father, and Terah blessed him and said to him, "Go in peace."

Abram journeyed from upper Lebanon and he took with him Sarai his wife, and his nephew Lot. Abram journeyed past Asshur on to Shechem, and dwelt near a lofty oak. Here Abram stopped to erect an altar, and do sacrifice unto Jah-el for the promise of the land. Abram continued in his quest, moving southward. He came to Hebron, a city, and dwelt there two years. Further southward he went to Bealoth; there was a famine in that land and so he went to Egypt. While in Egypt did the Pharaoh see Sarai, and was overwhelmed by her breathtaking beauty. He asked Abram concerning her and because of fear, for the Egyptians may have taken Abram's life concerning Sarai, he told Pharaoh she was his sister instead of his wife. Then did the monarch of Egypt take Sarai with intent of knowing her, but the Lord Jah-el sent plagues upon Pharaoh's house and his sorcerers told him that it was because of Sarai. Pharaoh gave Sarai back to Abram, indignant that Abram had not told him the truth concerning her, and Abram departed Egypt. Abram returned to Shechem; his dwelling place was bordered by Ai to the east and Bethel on the west. Here Jah-el spoke to the man Abram, again reassuring him of the promises concerning his seed and the land. Abram then moved, and settled in Hebron.

Abram and Sarai had no children of their own. Abram's nephew Lot, who had earlier parted company with his beloved uncle, now lived in the city of Sodom with his family. Jah-el had made mention on numerous occasions concerning Abram's seed, and had previously promised him an heir, but at age eighty-five there was no such offspring as yet for Sarai remained barren. In an act of desperation, Sarai told Abram to lie with her servant girl that she might conceive. Hagar was the name of the girl, and she was an Egyptian. Hagar became pregnant, and in the eighty-sixth year of his life bore him a son and he called his name Ishmael. Out of the loins of Ishmael, via his twelve sons, would come forth the Arab people.

When Abram was ninety-nine years of age, the Lord Jah-el spoke to him and made a covenant with him that the males of his children would be circumcised. This was an outward indication of the setting apart of the children of Abram to God's special purpose. Abram agreed to the covenant. Then the Lord Jah-el said something to Abram that made him dance for joy. Jah-el told him that he and his wife Sarai would have their promised son. He would be a miracle child, for now both Sarai and Abram were old. The life expectancy of men had diminished drastically after the falling of the flood's water. It was on this occasion that Jah-el changed the names of both Abram and Sarai. Abram's name meant *exalted father* but the Lord Jah-el changed his name to Abraham, which means *father of the multitude*. Sarai's name meant *my princess* but Jah-el changed it to Sarah, which means *princess*. On that same day did Abraham, Ishmael, and all the male members of Abraham's house become circumcised. When Abraham was one hundred years old a son was born unto him by Sarah, and they called his name Isaac. At the birth of Isaac I had been translated from the earth one thousand sixty-four years. Two thousand fifty-one years had elapsed since the creation of Adam.

Isaac grew to adulthood, and at age forty took to wife a young girl whose name was Rebecca. Ten years hence, at age six hundred, would Noah's son Shem die, and there would be great sorrow amongst the seed of Abraham for it was from Shem that Abraham was descended. Shem is the father of Abraham's line and down through the years would his descendants become known as Shemites, or Semites, the Semitic people. Ten years after Shem's death did Rebecca bear Isaac twin sons, and they called their names Esau and Jacob. Fifteen years after the birth of the twins did Abraham die at age one hundred and seventy-five. All that Abraham had attained in his lifetime was passed on to his son Isaac, including the covenant relationship and promises of the Lord Jah-el. The half brothers Isaac and Ishmael buried Abraham their father in the cave of Machpe'lah, in the field of Ephron, which is before Mamre, and the spirit of Abraham was transported to the holding place of Sheol in which flowed the bright and sparkling river of light.

CHAPTER 11

JACOB

And these are the generations of Isaac, Abraham's son. Isaac was forty years old when he took Rebecca to wife. Then Isaac entreated the Lord for his wife because she remained barren, and the Lord answered him and Rebecca conceived. But as the children within her grew, they began to struggle with one another and Rebecca inquired of the Lord Jah-el the reasoning. The Lord answered saying, "Two nations are in thy womb, and two manner of people shall be separated from thy bowels; and the one people shall be stronger than the other people; and the elder shall serve the younger." When her days to be delivered were fulfilled; behold, there were twins in her womb. The first came out red all over like a hairy garment; and they called his name Esau; after came out his brother, and his hand was grasped upon Esau's heel; and so his name was called Jacob.

Jacob was preceded by his brother Esau, so naturally Esau was bestowed the first-born birthright, but the Lord Jah-el had supernaturally decreed to Rebecca that her younger son would be the continuation of His covenant with

Abraham and Isaac. As the boys matured Esau grew to be an outdoorsman, a hunter, and favored by his father. Jacob grew to be a more refined man of culture and distinction, and favored by his mother. It occurred that on a particular day Esau, just back from a long and arduous hunting expedition, came famished to the tent of Jacob, and Jacob had simmering over his fire a savory stew. Esau begged his brother a bowl. But Jacob struck a proposition to Esau concerning his birthright, saying, "I will give you the stew if you pass to me your birthright as firstborn." Esau, irritated, retorted, "Jacob, I am famished near to death! What use is a birthright to me?" So it was that Jacob obtained the right of the firstborn, and Esau a bowl of stew.

When Isaac became an old man did his sight flee him, and his vision was reduced to shadows. It was the custom of the time when a father sensed the days of his life coming to a close that he call forth his firstborn to bless him, and pass on his legacy. Such a time had been determined by Isaac and so it was his intent to bestow his blessing upon Esau, though his wife had made known to him the revelation she had received of the Lord Jah-el. It was with the help of his mother, through deception, that Jacob was able also to obtain even Isaac's irrevocable blessing, and when Esau was made aware of what Jacob had done he plotted to kill him. This scheme was soon discovered by Rebecca and she told it to Jacob. With trickery anew she manipulated her husband to send Jacob away to Pa'dan-ar'am, to Laban her brother— the son of Bethuel the Syrian.

As Jacob was in flight to the house of Laban did night fall and he came to Bethel and camped there. He took some stones and piled them that he might use them as a rest for his back, and laid himself down to sleep. As he slept, Jah-el touched him with a vision in a dream. In his dream Jacob saw a ladder that extended from earth up into the heavens, and the angels of God were moving up and down the ladder, and at the very top of the ladder stood the Lord Jah-el Himself. Then the Lord said, "I am the Lord God of Abraham, and the God of Isaac. The land where upon thou liest, to thee will I give it and to thy seed. Your seed shall number as the dust of the earth, and thou shall spread out and take this land. I am with thee, and will keep thee; I will not leave thee, until I have done what I have spoken."

When Jacob awakened his spirit was cogitated and he mused, "Surely the Lord is in this place!" He arose, took the stones of his rest, set them up as a pillar, then poured oil on top of it, and vowed a vow, swearing, "Lord if You will be with me, and will keep me, and will provide for me, so that I come again to my father's house in peace, then shall You be my God."

Jacob continued on his way and eventually arrived at the house of Laban. Upon arrival Jacob instantly fell in love with Laban's youngest daughter Rachel, and soon bargained with Laban that he would work seven years for her hand in marriage. Laban agreed. At the end of the seven years did Laban adorn his daughter in heavy veils, covering even her eyes, and he told Jacob that this was the custom of his people regarding marriage, and that he could not see his bride in the light until the morning after the wedding. Jacob agreed, and was married conforming to the custom. When the ceremony and festivities were completed it was well into the night. Laban then escorted his daughter to the wedding tent as a sign indicating that she was no longer his, and the women of his household followed as well. Jacob remained behind with all the men of the camp and then shortly was escorted by them to the consummation quarters. Jacob eagerly bade them a good night in anticipation of the bride he had labored seven years to wed.

As the morning arose, bringing with it the first light, Jacob stirred, adoringly kissing she whom he thought was Rachel. To his utter horror were his eyes impacted by the vision before him—it was not Rachel he had wed but Leah, Rachel's older sister. Jacob was outraged, and began screaming his displeasure to the capacity of his lungs. Leah awakened and began to weep profusely in light of the unkind remarks of Jacob concerning her for Leah was not the beauty that Rachel was, neither did her eyes sparkle and dance. Jacob went sprinting from the tent clothed only in his undergarment with ill intent toward the person of Laban, cursing him for his trickery. Laban slowly emerged from his tent his men of valor already stationed, for Laban had anticipated Jacob's reaction. Jacob sneered at Laban demanding, "Why have you beguiled me Uncle?" Laban calmly replied, "It is against the custom of our land that a younger daughter should marry before the elder. I implore you Jacob to fulfill my daughter Leah, and in seven years time if you labor once more I shall also give you Rachel to wed." Jacob could only agree for it was Rachel he truly desired, and whatever it took he would possess her.

CHAPTER 12

THE NATION OF ISRAEL

In seven years time did Jacob also take Rachel to wife but in the meanwhile Leah had bore him four sons and their names were Reuben, Simeon, Levi, and Judah. Then Jacob began showing much more favoritism toward Rachel and continuously shared his bed with her, but through the course of time Rachel proved to be barren. Rachel became envious of her sister, and proceeded to ridicule Jacob that she had no child from him. This greatly angered Jacob, and he reminded her that the obvious fault was not in himself for Leah was ample proof. This was a devastating blow to Rachel and out of desperation she gave her handmaid Bilhah to Jacob as proxy, and Jacob knew her, and Bilhah bore him two sons, and he called them Dan and Naphtali. Because of the contentious aura that prevailed around Rachel Jacob began to find Leah much less unpleasant, and once more did he share his time with her. But Leah was not fertile as before and so as not to be upstaged by her sister, she gave her servant Zilpah to Jacob as her proxy. Then Jacob knew her and Zilpah bore him two sons, and he called them Gad and Asher.

Eventually tranquility settled over Rachel, for she prayed to the Lord Jah-el, and she believed in her heart that He had heard her. With this turn of events the relationship between Jacob and Rachel was reconciled, and once again did he know her. The Lord Jah-el graciously opened the womb of Rachel and she conceived, and bore a son and his name was called Joseph.

Shortly thereafter Leah became pregnant twice more and she bore sons, and their names were Issachar and Zebulon. But when Rachel conceived a second time and it came time for her delivery did she suffer complications, and Jacob's beloved Rachel died in childbirth. But the son she bore lived, and his name was called Benjamin. In all Jacob had twelve sons and out of these twelve sons would come the nation, the seed of Abraham that would become in number like the sands of the sea and the stars of the heavens.

It came to pass in length of time that Jacob left Laban, determined to return to the house of Isaac. Jah-el had prospered Jacob greatly within his service to Laban, and he was now a man of great wealth. Jah-el would indeed return him in peace to his father's house and He would heal the rift between him and his brother Esau. But while on his way home did a most momentous event take place, an occurrence that would have the most profound spiritual importance upon all future history, and would affect the entire world of all people, tribes and tongues, generation after generation.

Jacob had strategically sent his wives, his children, his household, and all his belongings ahead of himself, for he feared his brother Esau, and had no way of knowing what Esau's reaction would be to his return. Jacob was waiting by the brook Jabbok for a word from his servant as to whether it was safe for him to come to his father's house, when without warning a man appeared in the darkness and began to grapple with him. At first Jacob was convinced the worst had happened and Esau was assaulting him, for he was in a fight for his life. He wrestled with his assailant all night and then at the very slightest glimpse of dawn the Lord Jah-el permitted Jacob to perceive that this man was in fact not his brother Esau, but a messenger of heaven sent by Him. Jacob, always one at the ready to literally reach out and grab an opportunity, began to strive with the angel even more tenaciously. It was not that Jacob was stronger than the angel, but the angel was sent of Jah-el to test Jacob's persistence in obtaining a blessing. So the angel allowed Jacob to become the aggressor, wrestling with him a little while more. Then the angel insisted, "Release me, for the dawn is breaking and I must return." Jacob responded even more doggedly, "I will not release you, except you bless me." When the angel realized that Jacob would continue to the death if need be he simply touched Jacob's thigh, and dislocated his hip joint so that Jacob became disabled. But Jacob had a firm hold on the angel, and with still even more determination would not let go.

Jacob had passed the test, and the angel of the Lord ready with instruction of the blessing asked, "What is your name?" He replied, "Jacob." Then the angel said, "No more shall your name be called Jacob, but from this moment forward shall you be called Israel. For as a prince you have power with God, and with men."

From that day forward did Jacob become known as Israel and his sons as the twelve sons of Israel, and their offspring the twelve tribes of Israel. Out of Israel's twelve sons was birthed an entire nation called to the everlasting, and exclusive purpose of Jah-el. They became his chosen, the apple of his eye, and He became their husbandman, their

"I AM that I AM," their Adonai and Elohim. It was out of this people Israel that the Lord Jah-el would bring forth He who would bruise the head of the dark lord Lucifer—He who would conquer both death and Sheol—He who would redeem the future generations of *the called*—He who would become the very meaning of Abraham's seed blessing all nations—He who would be miraculously birthed into the world as *God on Earth.*

But then that is the continuation of His story.

EPILOGUE

Dear reader, I pray you've enjoyed and have been enlightened by this novel's journey.

Now that you know the primary cause and gist of God's plan for our salvation get a/your Bible and read the first thirty-two chapters of Genesis (again or for the first time), and see if it's much clearer to you. The Bible is God's written word to us, so please continue in its reading. I guarantee you the Holy Spirit will begin to reveal the rest.

Here is the prayer to pray if you are not yet one of *the called,* and wish to become so:

> **Heavenly Father, I confess myself a sinner in need of being washed in the blood of Your beloved Son Jesus Christ. I confess with my mouth and believe in my heart in Jesus as my only true Lord and Savior. I thank You that by the now indwelling presence of Your Holy Spirit within me, that I am now justified in Christ as one who has answered Your call.**

In Jesus' name, I pray. Thank You Father, Son and Holy Spirit.

Amen.

If you have just honestly, and earnestly, prayed this prayer let me be the first human to shout: Welcome into the kingdom of God! For Michael, Gabriel, Raphael, Uriel, and all the holy angels in heaven are already doing so (Luke 15:10).

By getting yourself into a good Bible-believing church under a pastor who both lives and preaches the unadulterated Word of God, the following is a scripture that over time you'll better learn to understand and appreciate.

And we know that all things work together for good to them that love God, to them who are ***the called*** according to His purpose. For whom He did foreknow, He also did predestinate to be conformed to the image of His Son, that He might be the firstborn among many brethren. Moreover whom He did predestinate, them He also ***called***: and whom He ***called***, them He also justified: and whom He justified, them He also glorified.

Romans 8:28–30

I think it safe to say that as a new babe in Christ you have no idea the power that your acceptance of Him as Savior has just placed within you, namely God the Holy Spirit. But you have the promise of Christ that the Holy Spirit will guide you (John 16:13). Believe this, as I know personally from twenty-five years of positive experience! Ask Him to direct you as to which church you should attend and He will make your way, and in time have all your questions answered too!

You also have in Scripture this promise as one who has answered His call; "God is faithful, by whom *ye were called unto the fellowship of His Son Jesus Christ* our Lord" (1 Cor. 1: 9).

Until we meet again, at such a time as it is the Lord's will for us to continue His story in **_Book 2_** of the trilogy: **_God on Earth_**, stay blessed my friend, and may you continue to seek His Word, will, and way for His call on your life. In Jesus' name—Amen.

Rahman Reuben
(life verse: Jeremiah 33:3)

CPSIA information can be obtained
at www.ICGtesting.com
Printed in the USA
LVHW031519180821
695588LV00004B/96